Advance Praise for *Truth and Other Fictions:*

"Eva Tihanyi's stories are exquisite paintings rendered in words—layered, textured, evocative—suggesting what is and the ghost-like presence of what was, and what might be. *Truth and Other Fictions* seduces with concision and a delicious tension between object/subject, interior/exterior worlds, and the possibilities and impossibilities of truth."
—Anna Camilleri, author of *I Am a Red Dress: Incantations on a Grandmother, a Mother and a Daughter*

Tihanyi's "work is concise and compressed, lucid and complex at the same time. Although the stories are short in length, they are deep and rich in references that reward a reader in much the same way that poetry does: there's more here than meets the eye...."
—Isabel Huggan, author of *The Elizabeth Stories, You Never Know* and *Belonging: Home Away from Home*

"Eva Tihanyi's stories embrace the paradox: 'Art is a lie that makes us realize the truth.' From stories of heart-breaking cracks in relationship, to fresh takes on such women as Billie Holiday and Mary Leakey, this is graceful writing that tells a truth only fiction can tell."
—Kim Echlin, author of *The Disappeared*

"Eva Tihanyi is a writer finely attuned to aesthetics, both in style and content. In her first collection of stories, *Truth and Other Fictions*, life itself moves towards art. Tihanyi involves us in that process expressed as luminous moments of mainly

contemporary female existence. Her women explore relationships and the sensual world, whether through painting, photography, music or personal makeover. Smoothly symbolic and often ironic, the deceptively random events in these brief narratives often make connections that transform the ordinary with lyrical insight."
—Patricia Keeney, author of seven books of poetry, including her *Selected Poems*, and the novel, *The Incredible Shrinking Wife*

"Lives become art as poetry weds prose in this evocative collection. With memoir-like intimacy, Tihanyi drops us into moments of truth and longing for the celebrated—Picasso, Leakey, Holiday, Brassaï—and the unknown. A muggy night 'as buttery as avocado,' a man as 'a crow, his dark feathers coy and menacing,' a 'scorched voice bare and absolute as bone:' Tihanyi reveals through telling details and surprising images. *Truth and Other Fictions* is a lyrical gift."
—Tricia Dower, author of *Silent Girl*

TRUTH

and Other Fictions

Also by Eva Tihanyi

Poetry

Wresting the Grace of the World

Restoring the Wickedness

Saved by the Telling

Prophecies Near the Speed of Light

A Sequence of Blood

TRUTH
and Other Fictions

STORIES BY

Eva Tihanyi

inanna poetry & fiction series

INANNA Publications and Education Inc.
Toronto, Canada

Canada Council   Conseil des Arts
for the Arts   du Canada    ONTARIO ARTS COUNCIL
CONSEIL DES ARTS DE L'ONTARIO

The publisher gratefully acknowledges the support of the Canada Council for the Arts and the Ontario Arts Council for its publishing program.

The publisher is also grateful for the kind support received from an Anonymous Fund at The Calgary Foundation.

Library and Archives Canada Cataloguing in Publication

Tihanyi, Eva, 1956-
    Truth and other fictions / Eva Tihanyi.

(Inanna poetry and fiction series)
ISBN 978-0-9808822-6-1

    1. Women — Fiction. I. Title.
II. Series: Inanna poetry and fiction series

PS8589.I53T78 2009   C813'.54   C2009-900994-3

Cover artwork: Barbara Bickel, "I Have Returned," mixed media collage on canvas, 30" x 26", 1995.
Cover design by Val Fullard
Interior design by Luciana Ricciutelli

Printed and bound in Canada

Inanna Publications and Education Inc.
210 Founders College, York University
4700 Keele Street
Toronto, Ontario, Canada M3J 1P3
Telephone: (416) 736-5356 Fax (416) 736-5765
Email: inanna@yorku.ca
Website: www.yorku.ca/inanna

To Barbara Fennessy and Darlene Hareguy
with love and gratitude.

Contents

Truth is what most contradicts itself in time.

—Lawrence Durrell

Green Is the Most Difficult Colour

Art is never chaste.
—Pablo Picasso

There is no abstract art. You must always start with something. He said this more than once and today, as I think of him on my seventy-sixth birthday, which also happens to be the opening of yet another retrospective of his work, I do so in terms of many *somethings*. I recall him in particulars, and it surprises me still, how being his model — his amusement even if only for a few short months — marked me.

He also said: *If there was a single truth, you couldn't make a hundred paintings of the same subject.* A hundred women, one man. A hundred truths. No truth at all. And so you start with something. One woman, one man.

I had just turned sixteen when I was sent on my first errand to his studio. It was an unseasonably warm Parisian May, the parks verdant with spring, the flourishing trees home to the calls of sparrows, thrush and warblers, blackbirds and nightingales. My father, who had shifted his small art supply business from London to Paris after my mother died the preceding year, had asked me to make a special delivery. He would ordinarily have made this delivery himself, given how important the painter was and that it was the man's first purchase — a substantial one — from my father. But today my father had legal matters regarding my mother's estate to attend to, and he asked me to go instead.

"He's a famous artist," he warned. "He could be good for business, so be on your best behaviour. And for God's sake, don't stare at him!" (My father had warned me more than once that my direct way of looking at people would one day invite trouble.) "And" — at this point he paused, brushing his eyes up and down me with an embarrassed flicker — "be careful."

He cautioned me a lot in those days. Perhaps it was only his role now as dual parent — both mother and father — that made him so attentive to my behaviour, but maybe he also sensed my growing need for adventure. My headstrong character he already knew.

When the short, deeply-tanned man opened the door, I couldn't help staring. He was wearing only black shorts which revealed his muscular body, strong shapely legs. He was compact in that tightly packed way that hints at tremendous energy. His chest was covered with salt-and-pepper curls. The top of his head was bald, the white hair on each side cropped short. His face reminded me of an

African mask I had seen in one of my father's history books. The roundness of the face, the almost chiselled quality of the features, the cheek lines deeply gouged. The dark magus eyes prominent and intense.

He stood in the doorway, a serious jester, imposing yet oddly open. In his right hand he balanced a paintbrush between thumb and forefinger as if it were a cigarette. His small hands boasted neatly manicured nails and were not at all paint-stained.

He stared back. We were both bold, I fuelled by innocence, he by its opposite. I was tall for my age and fair, my adolescent awkwardness camouflaged by an unapologetic, unflagging curiosity. Even back then, I looked life in the eye. I must have been a surprise to him though, the blonde hair, the summery green dress, the bright cherry earrings (my favourites). He probably wondered how I could carry the heavy wooden box of paints up the stairs, and took it immediately from my hands. I must have looked in need of a rest for he invited me in and poured us each a glass of water. Then he began checking the paints one by one. He paused at some of them; when he said their names, they sounded like poetry. Alizarin crimson, cadmium yellow, cobalt blue, French ultramarine, rose madder genuine, dragon's blood, raw sienna, Winsor green.

"Green," he said as he unwrapped a tube of veridian, "is the most difficult colour. Many variations, hard to mix. It needs a little red to warm it up, bring out its possibilities. Take the colour of your dress, for instance. It has red in it." He pointed toward the corner. "Or look at that green-heart branch over there. Look at what a pale, yellowish green it is. Yes, that would not be an easy one."

Perhaps that's what he saw most clearly as I stood there in his studio for the first time: the challenge of green. He looked up suddenly and asked if I would sit for him.

I remember it well, that first sitting, more than I remember any of the others that followed.

There was no music so he created his own, danced at the centre of the room crowded with canvases and exotic debris. Outside, the world was the world, busy with its private and public wars. There, in that bright windowed space, there was only a small Spanish man with a self as big as Spain. A country of contrasts, intense lights and darks, sun and shadow, the comic and the tragic daily intertwined. I sat in my difficult green dress watching him preside with impish nonchalance over the cavernous room in whose every corner lurked unexpected riches: oddly shaped bottles, musical instruments, discarded metal, old tools. With the amused benevolence of a man who has just outwitted someone, he held up piece after piece of accumulated bounty for my inspection. A shard of glass. Such a spectacular red! A snail's shell. Such wonderful intricacy! An old pocket watch. A miracle, that such a little box could contain so much time.

The child in him seduced the child in me.

He worked fast, could finish a portrait in a day if he felt like it, but he did not finish my portrait, not for many weeks. He would keep adding to it, deleting from it, altering it in both large and small ways. In the meantime, he drew me over and over, made dozens of sketches, none of which seemed to satisfy him. I still wonder what happened to them, for I never once saw him discard anything he created. I suspect now that the drawings were merely excuses to have me come to the studio whenever he wanted me there. Whenever he wanted me.

He had visitors on many afternoons, and he loved to put people on, especially those he suspected of riding on the coattails of his celebrity. Over-zealous journalists were always fair game. He had gone so far as to acquire a matador outfit, but that was only one of his disguises. Sometimes he appeared in a black cape, a white Stetson, or a lime terry robe with matching slippers. For one female magazine writer, he donned a horizontally striped undershirt and white boxers. My own favourite was the plastic nose with the attached horn-rimmed glasses. I saw him conduct an entire interview once wearing this partial mask. *It is not what the artist does that counts, but what he is*, I heard him say. An ingenuous remark, I now realize, but profound to me then. Much later I came to learn as I modelled for others, some almost as famous as he, that what the artist *is* infuses what he does.

His dealer once called him *incorrigible*. I remember that because I had no idea what it meant and had to look it up. I wondered if you could learn to be incorrigible. It seemed an eminently desirable trait.

Everything. Passion. Two powerful words. He said he never looked for a subject because everything was his subject. His whole life was his passion. *I paint just as I breathe.* He loved colour for its own sake. Harlequins, the beach, Cézanne's apples. Children (as long as they didn't interrupt his work). Scorpions because they were his zodiac sign and therefore a positive omen. Birds, animals, Barcelona brothels. The vitality of the philodendron. Solitude but also the noise and dust of the bullfight. He even loved his own restlessness. And women, of course. Women, intricate as clocks, fascinating as flowers. What he liked was to test, tease, cajole, coerce — to prod emotion from them the way a schoolboy prods spasms from an earthworm. When he was fourteen, he completed a portrait of his aunt in one hour. He made Gertrude Stein sit over eighty times for hers—at least that's what I heard later.

He painted impulsively, intuitively, caressing, stroking, lashing out. He painted with his whole being, all the while embracing disorder. He considered disorder a fertile breeding ground for ideas. He believed that objects would attract more attention if not assigned a specific place, made me sit in different places in his studio each time I came. Once he even hung a picture crookedly so it would look out of place, force people into noticing it. *A picture lives only through him who looks at it.* OJO, he would write on envelopes, parcels, books. Eye. Pay heed.

More than anything else, he taught me how to see.

There were things that bothered him, of course. Rain, haircuts, thin women, travelling by plane, religious ceremonies. And blindness, his greatest fear. He also resisted discussing aesthetics. I heard a story once about three young Germans who visited his studio and asked him to explain his theory of art. He pulled a revolver from his pocket and fired several shots into the air. The Germans fled, wordless.

To displace. To put eyes between the legs, or sex organs on the face. To contradict. To show one eye full face and one in profile. My painting is a series of non sequiturs. He held the oppositions in himself in a precarious and complex balance. He was a violent, funny man, one who loved the sun but preferred to paint at night.

He liked his women light so they could shine against his darkness. Women, like flowers, had their seasons. He enjoyed watching them open into full bloom, and then he picked the petals one by one, delicately pulled off the leaves. Finally, he would break the stem, not always intentionally. He was as reckless in his relationships as he was in his art. *Academic training in beauty is a sham. Art is not the application of a canon of beauty but what the instinct and the brain can conceive beyond any canon. When we love a woman we don't start measuring her limbs. We love with our desires — although everything has been done to try and apply a canon even to love.* Cannon, he should have said, for there was violence in his love.

He liked opening boxes just to see what was in them, especially if they were gifts, wrapped and ribboned. He attacked them with the insatiable, excited curiosity of a child.

I gave him a box once, as a gift. I had acquired an unexpected streak of creativity in his company. It was near the end of our months together when I sensed I was being replaced, that his interest had shifted. I built him a suffering machine, a machine that suffered, for that is what he called women when he had had enough of them. I carefully took apart one of my old dolls—she had blonde curls and blue eyes that closed when she was laid flat — and reconstructed her. By the time I was finished, the doll had lost any semblance of her initial humanity. I had interchanged her legs and arms, cut her hair into a spiky bush, glued her eyes shut. She suffered, and obviously.

I hoped he would be angry when he opened the box, but he wasn't. He laughed, and drilled me with those masterful eyes. Made holes. Continued laughing. I couldn't bear the humiliation of his delight. And then, in one of his sudden shifts, he softened, and was a lover once again. Embraced me tenderly, patted my head as if I were a little girl, slipped his hand between my legs, soothing, caressing. Praised me for what he called my fierce precociousness.

I overheard him, not long after he had first met me, telling the art dealer Kahnweiler: "That hair, that skin. I will paint her. I will show her to herself." To which Kahnweiler said: "She will hate you for it." *With me, a picture is a sum of destructions. I make a picture, and proceed to destroy it. But in the end nothing is lost; the red I have removed from one part shows up in another.*

Sometimes when I sat there hour after hour watching him watching me I felt hedged in, confined by his vision. I was nothing more than a reflection in his eyes. If he closed them, I would cease to exist. And yet, I did not grow jaded. In my stillness there was invisible movement. Spiritual photosynthesis. He did not know it, but I was absorbing his power.

I order things in accordance with my passions. What a sad thing for a painter who loves blondes but denies himself the pleasure of putting them in his picture because they don't go well with the basket of fruit! I put in my pictures everything I like. So much the worse for the things—they have to get along with one another. His entire personal universe operated as if it were a painting into which he threw disparate elements just to see what they might do. People, places, objects in huge accidental configurations of disarray. To him, a pleasing emotionally incendiary chaos. To others, a disaster.

It wasn't long after the doll incident that he introduced me to his new mistress.

We all know that art is not truth. Art is a lie that makes us realize the truth. The painting he did of me no longer exists. I know this because I destroyed it during my last afternoon at his studio. Slashed it to shreds with his sharpest canvas cutter. Hated him at that moment, as Kahnweiler had predicted I would. I still remember the clock parts entwined with snail shells in the background, my hardly recognizable face, one eye full face, one in profile, and the green dress, the green not quite exact. And what I remember most clearly is the touch of red near the heart.

No Ordinary Eyes

It is late in the spring evening, but the cobblestones still glisten with afternoon rain. Gyula Halász leaves the Hôtel des Terrasses where he has recently taken up residence, and makes his way to the Boulevard du Montparnasse. He will stop in at the Dôme and the Rotonde, before he heads off on his nocturnal roamings, which involve, inevitably, veering from familiar routes. He has slept all day, feels fearless and curious and intensely awake. His father's generosity has ensured his comfort. His rent is paid, his clothes are clean. He has francs in his pocket. Also in his pocket: another letter from his mother, begging him to come home. Her words press against his heart like a hand.

So far 1930 has been good to Gyula Halász. A new year, a new decade, and he has begun to create himself in the City of Light. If only his parents could see his happiness. If only they could trust in his success, which is close, so close. He cannot possibly return to Brassó no matter how much they miss him, how fervently they insist. He can sense it, the fate he has chosen, waiting for him. Perhaps around the very next corner, in the next photograph.

He doesn't mind that the equipment he carries is cumbersome: Voigtlander camera, tripod, only 24 plates because of their weight. He wants to capture what remains visible in the darkness when the only light comes from the moon and the gas streetlamps, the boisterous windows of bars and cafés, hotels and brothels. He has been gathering the city for months, has filled himself up with it, believes that photographs are the only way he can reveal what he now contains. He wanders among the night denizens, the drunks and derelicts, the prostitutes and wealthy partiers, the bakers preparing morning baguettes, the workers polishing tramlines. He is a camera gypsy in search of poetry, carnivals of light which flare in unexpected corners, down side streets, at the hidden ends of alleys. Gyula Halász. Jules Fisherman. Fisherman of Jewels. The camera nets him fortuitous prizes: the open gutter snaking its way across the deserted street, cats greeting each other by tall wrought-iron gates, patterns of shadow crisscrossing garden-walks and cemeteries, barges resting on the Seine.

Gyula Halász casts his sight on everything, tells his friends that objects have raised him, finally, to their own level. And when he shows them his photographs, they understand what he means. Paperclips, sewing needles, drawing pins are things of involuntary beauty. A thimble is a sculpture. The arrangement of five matches on a page of typed text: compelling. Every object radiates a secret life, exudes a dazzling sense of itself, which his eyes reveal to him. The seeing makes his heart beat faster. Such ruthless joy! He vows to spend every day of his life in the practice of amazement. If only his parents could recognize this force in him, powerful as a waterfall.

No one who meets Gyula Halász can ignore his eyes. Like his mother's, they are prominent and orb-like, the whites completely encircling the black pupils. This gives them a disconcerting openness which many find intimidating, some mystical. A few discern the visage of a slightly manic but wise turtle who studies them without blinking. He is never the first to turn away.

Gyula Halász peers through the window of the Café Bijou, where he has never before been, considers going inside for a *café crème*. He will write a long-overdue letter to his parents. He wishes his mother would stop pleading with him to come home. He has tried to explain his reasons, but she cannot comprehend them. Seeing changes things, and he does not want to re-vision where he is from. He cherishes the original picture, which he has fixed irrevocably in his mind.

This is true, but he knows it is not the whole truth. What he doesn't say: it might be dangerous, he loves his parents too much. All forms of love are hooks, and he cannot allow himself to get caught. If he does, he might end up in Brassó forever. He has invited his parents to visit him in Paris, but he will not go to them. He will not return. Not now, not later. Eventually, when he is ready, when he becomes Brassaï, he will honour his birthplace. *From Brassó*, his name will announce. That will be enough.

Although his French is now fluent, it still gives him pleasure to write in Hungarian. *Jol vagyok*, he assures his parents in every letter. I am fine. He tells them that he has renounced whatever is quiet, mediocre, inauthentic; that he wants to live a grand life, one in which his curiosity will be the guiding passion. With his eyes, he will feast on the world. He is willing to take risks to accomplish this. He refuses to sail on safe, idyllic rivers but chooses instead the ocean with its crests and troughs. *If you are impatient, if you, whom I love the most, want to get me to dry land by any means, how can I overcome the obstacles?* His father reads his letters over and over, savours them like victory. They are his father's own dreams brought to life on the page. His father does not admit this. His mother sighs. It's always good to get word from her son but how, where, did her Gyulus get these wild ambitions? She glances at her husband, his smiling face.

Inside the café, amidst the swirling smoke, a small girl, five or six perhaps, sits in a corner with only her doll for company. Although it is late, she does not seem tired. Her mother serves customers, prepares to finish work for the night. If the girl were to look up, she would see Gyula Halász, his inquisitive face, the relentless intensity of his stare. But she does not notice the man at the window, nor anyone. The doll has entirely captivated her. She stands it up; its eyes flip open. She lays it down; its eyes close. She performs this magic repeatedly, fascinated by the small spectacle. Gyula Halász watches her, the wonder of her wonder. This is the way he will photograph the city: with its eyes closed, its eyes open. Again, again. He feels a powerful delight surge within him. He does not go in, keeps walking.

There is no such thing as complete darkness. The world is a shimmering surface of contrasts, light and dark inseparable partners. Objects will themselves to be noticed. And if you look at anything long enough, it will start to change right before your eyes. Gyula Halász stands gazing at a cluster of enormous chestnut trees, the blossoms of which are like a thousand tiny chandeliers, radiantly white. One exposure will suffice. It will be long and require stillness. All he needs is the ambient light, the light already there. He will lure it in. He adds nothing but patience, the passage of time. He stands beside his tripod-mounted camera, cigarette balanced at the corner of his mouth, hands in his pockets; waits for the light to press itself slowly, gradually, onto the photographic plate. The blossoms become inverted grape clusters coated entirely in snow.

The following night Gyula Halász returns to the Café Bijou with his friend Dobó. He has come with intention. There is no sign of the little girl and her doll, and he is disappointed, but her mother is there. She glances up when the men enter bearing the bulky equipment, which this time includes a magnesium flash. Gyula Halász takes her in. Young, maybe twenty-five. Auburn hair, bobbed and crimped. Sleeveless V-necked black top and a black skirt. Red lipstick and red nail polish, exactly the same shade. It is warm in the café and her face shines. He introduces himself, learns her name is Thérèse. He tells her that he doesn't want to simply take her photograph. Rather, he would like her to help him create one. A photograph must be enticed, coaxed into being, and he would be honoured if she would join him in this endeavour. Charmed, she agrees.

Catching people is different from catching bridges, buildings, parks. People don't stay still, not even their faces. Especially not their faces. Ambient light is not enough; long exposures are impossible. A different form of patience is required, a different method. And so, Gyula Halász prepares his scenes precisely. He scripts the image, stage-manages reality into something more real, something greater than itself, and then waits to see what revelation will take the bait.

He often gets his friends to pose for him in various guises, as lovers or hoodlums or revellers. Tonight it is Dobó he has enlisted for this purpose. Dobó wearing his checkered cap and rakish grin, game always for anything. He is glad that Thérèse has agreed to take part but doesn't find her cooperation unusual. He has never had anyone refuse his photographic attention. He is convinced that there is no woman who, when given the opportunity, does not want to be seen. He decides that if his mother ever visits him, he will convince her to let him photograph her.

He will show her who she really is, and then, perhaps, she will finally understand him.

Gyula Halász asks the bartender to assist him by sparking the flash when he is signalled. He tells Thérèse and Dobó that they are to be lovers, seats them facing each other at a corner table where two mirrors intersect. The fact that there are mirrors pleases him. They will provide additional angles, the illusion of three dimensions, like being able to see the dark side of the moon when it is facing away. He places glasses of red wine on the table, one in front of Thérèse, one in front of Dobó. He directs them to smoke, talk, pretend that they are making up after a fight. When he finishes arranging them, he steps back, positions himself behind the camera.

As the minutes pass, Thérèse and Dobó slide into the roles Gyula Halász has assigned them. Gradually, however, they lapse into being whoever they might be if he weren't there at all. Their initial awkwardness fades, and they become forgetful. They forget about the other patrons, who have returned gradually to their own conversations. They forget about Gyula Halász, his camera, the bartender holding the flash. Their private selves begin to glimmer through their public poses. Gyula Halász feels the prickle of instinct, opens the shutter, covers the lens with his hat. Soon. The bartender watches intently, anticipating his cue.

It is when Dobó suddenly leans forward to kiss Thérèse that Gyula Halász removes the hat. In the exact instant the kiss is over, he signals the bartender. A burst of flash, a puff of white smoke, the room suddenly brilliant with illumination. There is a small collective gasp as people startle into awareness. He closes the shutter. The image is caught like a momentary flicker of a fish as it breaks through the surface of the water.

Gyula Halász doesn't allow anyone to touch his negatives. He develops and prints each one himself in the makeshift darkroom he has created in a corner of his hotel room. He is convinced that the photograph is not in the negative but in the print created by the photographer. It is about enlarging, cropping, discovering the core image in what the camera was allowed to frame.

He makes several prints of Thérèse and Dobó. The final version does not show Dobó at all. There is only Thérèse in profile, sitting at the table, cigarette in hand, wine glass in front of her. Her eyes are still closed. She is a woman savouring, though trying hard not to, the aftermath of an unanticipated kiss. In the mirror behind her, the photographer and his camera are visible, and behind him, holding her doll upright so it too faces the mirror, the wholly unforeseen: Thérèse's little girl.

For Gyula Halász, a miracle is always invited but never expected. Endlessly, the light streams in, gracing with surprise all that it touches. In this spirit, he continues his explorations. His shutter opens and closes as night after night the city gives itself up to him. He is a purveyor of truths pulled from the world despite their slipperiness. His eyes hold presents for the future; in

photographs, he will send them. Finally, his mother and
father will see. Above them too, the stars will explode
like diamonds.

Body and Soul

The hot sun bears down on Oludvai Gorge, the early morning coolness past as the hour edges toward eleven. Mary Leakey, in short-sleeved shirt and khakis, has been wandering alone amid the scree for hours. She shifts her wide-brimmed straw hat to a better angle against the painfully bright light, catches the silhouette of a vulture searching for prey. By noon the glarc will make distinguishing fossils from mere stones almost impossible. Already the black-and-white of the two Dalmatians cavorting along beside her seems more intense than it was.

Half a world away, the heat rises slowly, the muggy New York night still buttery as avocado. In a room at the Metropolitan Hospital, Billie Holiday lies in a medley of dreams, dying. It is all finally becoming clear to her, each moment as crystalline as a perfect note. She has never felt more lucid. A sleight-of-heart, this sudden memory avalanche, and before the final forfeit there are still astonishments. At first a black sound that is the absence of sound, a voracious silence, then she's standing in front of the microphone, hears her own voice singing itself into existence. And then the applause, always the applause, which makes her feel both loved and afraid, carefree and melancholy. It has become her trademark, this sad insouciance.

*   *   *

Mary thinks of her artist father, long deceased, how he would have admired the dogs' incongruity against the background of stratified rock. He would have loved the steep cliffs and acute sky, the profound mind-calming silence which makes true hearing possible. She is sure that he, too, would have heard the dry winds whisper across the Serengeti Plains, winds bearing the haunting bark of zebras and a thousand hooves thrumming across the grasslands. She misses him, is keenly aware of all the years since his passing. Senses the eons that have brought her here, the volcanic eruptions, the shifting of faults, the process of erosion. The ancient sediment under her feet shelters a buried human narrative. She intends to uncover it.

Swaggering toward a front table where Billie has made sure a chair has been saved, Louis, tall and dapper, smoothes his thin moustache. He's wearing his widest ate-the-canary grin, dimples showing, as well as the expensive new topcoat she recently bought for him. He's late again, which makes her feel like crying. But she doesn't, she sings instead. *My man don't love me, treats me awful mean. My man he don't love me, treats me awful mean. He's the lowest man I've ever seen.* Her white gown is tight, a tourniquet, holding her together. She is assured by the grip of her high-heeled white shoes, the fragrant weight of the white gardenias in her hair. She's a lady, and she's fine. Louis is fine too, a fine black cat. But he's in a bad mood tonight; she knows the signs. She glances at his hands, sees him turn his heavy diamond ring around. That way it won't leave a mark on her face later. He always makes sure he's smiling when his fist connects.

* * *

Mary hates rules, always has. Was expelled from two different convent schools. After that, learned to pilot gliders, identify archaeological artefacts, draw meticulously. She has always favoured rebellion, choice. Shunned mediocrity. Danger has never frightened her. Her mother cannot get used to this. Her mother cannot get used to Louis either. She thinks him dashing, handsome, and charming, all of which are questionable traits in a husband. His boyishness does not convince her. His ambition does not convince her. She does not like his moustache nor the fact that he's ten years older than her daughter. Most of all, she does not like his history, the detail that he was already married and left his wife pregnant when he ran off with Mary. The only thing certain about Louis, she tells Mary, is that he doesn't doubt his own importance, not for a minute, not ever.

Billie, too, makes choices, although she doesn't think about them. She continues to choose Louis, the act of choice itself a form of freedom.

* * *

Mary pours a whisky, lights a Cuban cigar, and puts her faith in work, the harder the better. She knows that scientists are lucky to be remembered for even one contribution past their lifetime, and interpretation is not what she wants to be remembered for. She is content to leave that to others. What she yearns for is the action of discovery. Description and documentation. Accuracy. These are the things that count. Her legacy will be in the finding.

Billie dreams and dreams. Louis is a crow, his dark feathers coy and menacing. His predatory heart is forever ravenous; there is never enough food, never enough food. His beak pecks away at her frayed life that can no longer be mended. Thread by thread, he undoes her. In his glossy black plumage, she sees herself reflected. She is growing smaller, unravelling. But then he begins his easy touching, its intimate rhythm a delicious euphoria, and she forgets everything. *I am a fool to want you.*

* * *

Even when Mary is not alone, she demands quiet at her sites. She herself speaks only when necessary. The workers want music; they want to sing. She forbids them even to talk, if it can be avoided. She believes in the focusing power of movement without words. And so the workers are hushed but resentful. The only sounds: bone bits shaking in sieves, boots crunching on stone. Today Mary experiences a rare pleasure: hours of total solitude, no human voice at all, not even her own.

Billie struggles to breathe. In her dream she's back at the Phoenix Theatre, attempting to rise from her ashes one last time. *When you walk out there and open your mouth, you never know what's going to happen.* Bright as a valentine at the back of the room, her mother's red velvet bird-of-paradise hat. And there behind it, Lester Young, the Pres, holding his tenor saxophone as far out in front of him as he can, trying to give it more space, more air. He plays for pleasure, happens upon grace, the sweetness of it lingering in the phrasing, the nuances between notes. But the Pres is dead, just as her mother is dead. Billie knows this, and more, much more. She knows she will be next, has no appetite for anything but gin; has had more than a quart already. The elbow-length gloves cover the needle marks but can't hide her upper arms, which are alarmingly scrawny like matchsticks. She is a tattered bird, too feeble almost to stand, the weak light hard on her face. But feeling has always sung her, not the other way around, and so she sings—badly, but still she sings, her scorched voice bare and absolute as bone.

* * *

Mary knows, and one day she will write it down: *You dig for one thing and you find something quite different. There are so many stories to be discovered. And every one you find is different from the one you expected.*

Louis isn't the first in the flock of crows, but he is the last. His powerful wings cast a smothering shadow. In Billie's dream, the music gets faster, louder, the applause is endless. She is feverish, breathless, buried in her mink coat, her mother's embrace, the thick bar smoke. Flight, not possible.

* * *

It's always a surprise. A sudden whiteness catches Mary's eye. An unusual whiteness, perhaps a trick of the light. She crouches down, carefully brushes away the earth to reveal part of a skull. She brushes away more. Gently, gently. The base of a jaw appears, and embedded in it two molars four times the size of her own. They look — dare she think it? — human. She takes one deep breath after another, tries to rein in her excitement. She marks the spot with her hat, weights the hat with a rock, walks as quickly as she can back to the Land Rover. She wishes the winding path out of the gorge wasn't so treacherous. Even before she reaches the shoulders of the canyon, she pushes down hard on the accelerator.

The heat is heavy, smothering. Billie opens her mouth for the last time. There are no words. There is only a breath, silence.

* * *

It will take Mary fifteen minutes to get back to the camp where Louis lies ill with the flu. "I've got him! I've got him! I've got him!" she says, dancing from one foot to the other. Her pale eyes have given up their usual steeliness, are intense as blue flames. Louis is feverish. He thinks he's dreaming.

"*Who* have you got, Mary?"

"I've got our Dear Boy! I've got our earliest man."

Billie Holiday dies at 3:20 a.m. A poet will write of seeing her face on the front page of the *New York Post*. Many will mourn. Some will attempt biographical analysis. Louis McKay will consider his fortune.

* * *

It will take Mary eighteen months to piece together the four hundred pieces of her skull puzzle. In the meantime, Louis Leakey will give interviews, travel to conferences, acquire grant money, preen in front of his peers. He will father all the happy enterprise that follows. She will choose to remain in the background, will proceed with diligence, collecting fossils and facts, facts and fossils. Doing what she does best: finding.

Billie will continue to sing herself into the future, her voice a fact, a fossil. An elusive artefact, never completely found.

The New York Times Cook Book

Wine stimulates conversation, sharpens the wit and brings forth all.... —*The New York Times Cook Book* (1961)

"Here. Take this, and pour us both a glass of wine," you say, handing me a shoebox as you surface from the basement to check on the lasagna. You make it from scratch with authentic ingredients from the Italian grocery store, and the rich garlicky aroma is making me hungry.

"So what's in the box?"

"I'll show you." You pull the lid off to reveal a jumbled pile of photographs. Since we've bought a house together and are moving into it soon, we've both been busy ridding ourselves of detritus from our previous lives. I, myself, have already unloaded the miscellany left over from two previous husbands. This shoebox, you tell me, contains the last of yours, pictures of ex-partners mixed in with pictures of long-deceased pets, friends whose names you can no longer remember, unidentified landscapes from an assortment of summer vacations.

But there are other things too, among them assored

group shots, several of which are of a dinner party. "The party that changed my life," you say, as you pass the picture to me. Everyone looks past forty, except for you and another young woman. "Who's this?" I ask. You smile fondly. "Gillian. She was a good friend; really my only friend in those days. She was a grad student like I was. Bright and funny, and a lot more confident than the rest of us. She was single and knew how to have a good time. People called her unconventional. I think she just had more of a sense of who she was than most women did back then. Certainly more than I ever did."

Gillian is seated next to a large man in a navy-blue suit — all of the men are in suits — sporting a flamboyant red tie. John Cox, the American writer. He was a celebrity in the sixties though no one hears much about him these days.

"Amazing to think about it now, considering how inexperienced I was," you say, "but Richard had me taking care of many such social events."

"Wasn't he worried that something might go wrong?"

"He didn't think about it. Just assumed that I'd do what had to be done — what he *wanted* done. Lucky for him I was a quick learner."

You smile again, and as I refill our glasses, I can't resist the persistent tug of curiosity. "So, how did the party change your life?"

You are twenty-four, in your spotless kitchen on a Thursday evening in March, tall, slim, leggy, your blonde hair hanging past your shoulders. Brigitte Bardot with brains, Richard liked to call you when you were still his student, although you really didn't resemble her at all.

Your intelligence, which you tried hard to downplay in front of others as was the custom of the times, could not have been easily ignored. It would have been your eyes that most betrayed it, their warm hazel gaze direct and steady, full of inquisitiveness and already a hint of sadness. Back in those days you used them to examine books far more intently than you did men, and so you didn't examine Richard closely enough, took him at face value. He was, after all, Dr. Richard Rittenhouse, professorial Englishman, who had done his undergraduate work at Cambridge and his Ph.D. at Harvard. He was well-travelled, knew fine points about things you had never heard of. He was the sort of Richard who didn't allow anyone to call him Dick, although from what you've told me, the diminutive would have suited him well. In short, he was the sort of scholar that Canadian universities loved so well in those days: from somewhere more important than Canada. He spoke the Queen's English. When he married you, it was yet another form of empire building. You were a virgin colony to be conquered and civilized. This did not occur to you until later, however.

In the beginning you were completely taken by Richard, a practiced purveyor of charm. He praised your work, told you how he had singled you out right away as someone special. Because Richard didn't wear a wedding ring, you had no idea he was married, and you didn't think to ask. Those were the days when you still believed that what you saw was what you would get. When he asked you to meet him for coffee to discuss the possibility of your becoming his teaching assistant the following term, you believed that that is why he wanted to see you. Despite your scholarship-winning brilliance, nothing in your small-town south-western Ontario upbringing had prepared you for the sophisticated deceptions of a worldly, middle-aged womanizer like Richard. You thought of him in much the same way you thought of your father: a remote man to be respected, admired, and trusted. You basked in his attention. He made you feel desired. You didn't find out until after you had slept with him that he was married. You might not have found out for months had it not been for a phone call from his wife, Jan, who had apparently been tipped off by one of his more vindictive colleagues. She, of course, eventually divorced him, but it wasn't as easy in those days as it is now. You figure Richard must have bought her off to get her to cooperate, move things along faster. Scandal threatened — there was talk that he wouldn't be granted tenure — so he thought it best to marry you as soon as possible. He was always good at damage control.

On the day of the John Cox dinner party, you had already been married for more than two years. I can picture it as you tell the story: you and Richard in the kitchen, you planted in front of him, your feet apart, your weight evenly balanced, a leftover habit from your basketball days. A confrontational stance if one wanted to look carefully, but Richard doesn't. He's too busy telling you that he has invited people for Saturday dinner, and there's a list of pick-ups you must attend to: his beige suit from the cleaners, a copy of Cox's latest novel so he can skim it before Saturday (also so that he has a copy for him to sign), ink for the Mont Blanc pen, a new corkscrew.

This is the way it has been throughout your marriage. It was the way it was with Jan, too. At least that's what one of the other faculty wives told you. Richard assumes that he will say and his wife will do. The fact that you are working on your doctorate in English literature is irrelevant. On Saturday, your role as the host's wife will be to cook well, converse courteously (but not too cleverly), smile often (but not too much). Your most important responsibility, however, will be to create envy in Richard's colleagues by looking sensational and gazing at Richard with adoration, your attractiveness thereby creating the illusion of his.

"Gilt by association," I can't resist interjecting.

You tell me that you're convinced Richard set out to create his dream wife even before the ink was dry on the marriage certificate, a classic case of Pygmalion syndrome. His wedding gift to you was an upscale set of pots and pans, and a copy of *The New York Times Cook Book*. This was to be your domestic bible. He figured that since you couldn't cook, you ought to learn from the best, and who better than Craig Claiborne, the most revered food critic in the entire United States. You didn't feel at all offended—after all, even Virginia Woolf had gone to cooking school after she married Leonard. But, you ruefully admit, unlike you, Virginia had the unconscious good sense to cook her wedding ring into a suet pudding.

The list for Saturday night is typical of Richard's taste in guests: three of his University of Toronto colleagues sporting wifely wives, and John Cox, who is from Boston and sounds like the Kennedys. The fact that his most recent novel was reverentially reviewed in *Time, Newsweek,* and *The New York Times Book Review* has given the upcoming dinner an extra edge. Athough he'd never admit it, Cox's fame intimidates Richard, and he hurls more instructions than usual, his British accent emphatic, a sign that he is anxious. *Make sure you use the Royal Doulton and the Waterford. Make sure the silver is polished and the linen napkins are ironed. Get a good white burgundy — Pouilley-Fuissé or Le Montrachet* (as someone who has, since high school, consistently aced her French classes, you can't help but wince at his pronunciation) *if you can find either, which is unlikely in this town. Try anyway. Pick up a bottle of Remy Martin for after. And invite Gillian. She's smart and she's gorgeous. Fox will love her.*

You tell him that Gillian is heading off to California in the morning and will probably not be available. He tells you to invite her anyway. You listen carefully to all of Richard's instructions, have what he calls a "rat-trap memory" so don't need to write anything down. You ask him about the main course. He's chosen white wine, so he must already have something in mind. Would he like Poulet Marengo or maybe Breast of Chicken en Papillote? Or perhaps the Indonesian Satay Kambing Madura? He settles on one of his own personal favourites, the Fish Fillets Bonne Femme, stating that the satay would probably be too spicy for all concerned, and he's heard that John Cox prefers fish over meat. *Make Angels on Horseback as an appetizer,* he says. *That one isn't in the cook book,* you say, having often and meticulously studied its pages. *But you've made it before,* he insists. *No, I haven't. It must've been Jan.* He doesn't miss a beat. *Well then don't worry about it. Make Oysters Rockefeller. And dessert.*

You don't tell him your paper on appearance versus reality in the fiction of Nabokov is due on Monday. The last time you tried to explain that you couldn't entertain his colleagues because you had schoolwork to do led to the worst fight you'd ever had, during which Richard declared that even after you completed your Ph.D., he would be the professor and you his wife. Your role would be to support *his* career, not begin one of your own. This was not at all your idea of things, and thus was planted a seed that would lie dormant through three years and the birth of a child but would flower, eventually, into a life without Richard.

You are relieved that Fish Fillets Bonne Femme is not one of the more exotic or difficult dishes you've cooked. It's basically a matter of baking sole in mushrooms, cream, and white wine. He could have asked for bouillabaisse. Or Homard à l'Absinthe, which would involve live lobsters. You'll have to bake the sole in the fanciest casserole dish though to dress it up a bit, and be sure to have an extra-extravagant dessert. Maybe that lovely milk and egg concoction you surprised him with last month. Floating Island. Sugary clouds of egg white suspended on a lake of liquid custard. But no, that would be too much dairy for one meal. Cherries Jubilee, which you had for the first time in Paris on your honeymoon, might be better. It's a dessert Richard likes, so you've made it often.

Your honeymoon had been your first time in Europe — your first time out of Ontario, in fact — and you were overwhelmed. Richard delighted in your inexperience. He took you to expensive restaurants, enjoyed telling you that the rind did not need to be removed from the Camembert and that no, the wine glasses did not need to be filled to the brim. An entire dinner could become a lecture, and anything was fair game: the style of the salad fork, the weave of the tablecloth, the design of the menu, the architecture of the room. And then there would be the walks, imperious Richard in all his pedantic glory parading you around on his arm as if you were a Stradivarius umbrella while he pointed out sights, gave elaborate histories. You laugh about it now, laugh at your own naiveté, your ignorance in the ways of the world, the world of men. But back then you were simply enthralled to be with him, distinguished professor, successful older man.

The dinner party does not end well. Your eyes crinkle with amusement now as you share the memory. Gillian does attend, and there you are, the group of you, around the dining room table, candles lit, classical music in the background. Pictures are taken. Everyone is smiling amiably. You have all had far too much wine (it ended up being a lowly Mouton Cadet) and are now into the cognac. Richard, who insists on lighting the Cherries Jubilee, also insists that only good cognac will do and pontificates on the merits of Remy Martin.

You don't quite know what happens. You meet Gillian's eyes and are suddenly overcome with giddiness, can't resist commenting on the jubilant cherries, their lusciousness, their heat, their sweet red darkness. *Courvoisier.* The sensual French rolls off your tongue like a purr. *I prefer Courvoisier.* You pause. *On my cherries.*

The room is suddenly quiet. Everyone except John Cox has been in your company many times before, but no one has ever heard you speak like this. Cox shifts his interest from Gillian beside him to you across the table. *Why don't you come and park on my lap, honey?* he says. Before you can answer, Gillian does an extraordinary thing. She rises from her chair and walks around the table to where you are seated. Then she takes your face in her hands and kisses you, slowly, tenderly, on the mouth. There is a dream-like quality to this kiss, as if there were no audience, as if it were not really happening. It is a kiss that will change your life, once you understand it, but this will take a long time. At the moment you cannot allow yourself to think about it. You are stunned and tired and more-than-slightly drunk, and what you want most is for everyone to go home.

Richard, who has been gaping like a fish, continues to gape. One of the guests says it's late, time to go. Everyone murmurs their agreement. The farewells are fast and efficient, a relief to all. Both Richard and you, in a supreme act of joint denial, pretend — and will continue to do so for the rest of your marriage — that the incident never happened. Whether anyone says anything about it to him afterward, you will never know. No one says anything to you.

You head to the kitchen to check on the lasagna. When you return, you're holding your tattered copy of *The New York Times Cook Book*. It is food-stained and spineless, held together by a large elastic band. From between page 264 and 265 you slide a postcard.

"Gillian sent me this from California. A thank-you note."

It is a photograph of a Courvoisier bottle and a bowl of cherries glued onto a blank card. On the back, nothing but the words *I prefer.*

Words and Music

Seeing it as it is today, it's hard to imagine Budapest as it was when I was born, several months before the October Uprising of 1956. That event, like all such events, has been reduced by the passage of time, its essence relegated to old news photographs: students hurling Molotov cocktails at Russian tanks or the massive statue of Lenin toppled, its severed head heavy on the ground, only the boots left standing. Many of those who were there don't want to speak of it, don't want to be reminded. Take my parents, for instance. They refused to discuss their harrowing haycart escape across the border or what it felt like to leave me, their six-month-old daughter, behind. They settled for silence and allowed words to fail them. This, as I grew older, I vowed I would not do. I would let words *save* me instead.

The Berlin Wall has been down for over fifteen years, the Soviet Union dissolved, the euro accepted. Cars jostle for parking spaces, horns blare on the Danube-straddling bridges. Hungarian menus boast items such as shrimp in lemon-mango coulis and risotto with Portobello mushrooms and gorgonzola. Much has changed though if you know where to look, you will still see bullet holes in the old central city apartment buildings. The Liszt rhapsodies, gypsy violinists, aroma of paprika and onions — these remain, as does the regal architecture, imposing and elegant. And there, on one of the city's most impressive thoroughfares, the wide and stately Andrássy *út*, stands the equally impressive neo-Renaissance opera house — the Hungarian State Opera House as it is officially known.

My grandmother loved opera, and I loved my grandmother in whose care I was left for the first six years of my life. It is because of these facts that I find myself on this warm June evening at what she used to call simply *az opera ház*, the opera house, as if it were the only one on Earth. Long after she had immigrated to Canada, she spoke of the balconied façade with its statues of great composers; the seemingly endless walls of ornate paintings; the grand marble staircases with their red carpeting. And more even than the indisputable splendour of the place, she praised the soaring drama of the music that animated it. *Tosca, La Traviata, Rigoletto*. The names sounded like exotic foreign places, musical cities that I, as a southern Ontario teenager raised on sixties rock-and-roll, had no interest in visiting. Opera itself seemed forbidding and meaningless, something to make fun of, to mimic in a high falsetto with friends. It belonged to the old, to people who did not know how to dance, or did not want to.

Sitting here now in the front row of a second-storey box, ten minutes before the performance of *La Bohème* is to start, I try to take it all in. My grandmother did not exaggerate: the grand horseshoe-shaped auditorium is splendid. A circular Lotz fresco, *Olympus,* adorns the ceiling, from which hangs an enormous bronze chandelier, tiered like a wedding cake. The walls are decorated with gold.

I glance down at the program, am surprised at how the familiar English letters form Hungarian words that I am able to understand. It's much more laborious than reading English since I've had so little practice, but this makes it seem even more magical, like gradually comprehending a code. A genetic code, because it feels as though the words are in my cells.

Despite a lifetime of English, and despite the fact that I left Hungary before I started school, Hungarian remains within me, a current flowing deep in the strong English river. *Út:* road. *Hid:* bridge. *Viz:* water. *Fa:* tree. *Virág:* flower. *Járda:* sidewalk. *Ablak:* window. *Ajto:* door. I can call forth the words at will, hundreds of them, can name everything, speak with anyone. This power is formidable and reassuring. Although English is the language in which I think, Hungarian is my Eden language, the language in which I first learned the world. And although it's in English that I know desire, passion, and tenderness, my love for my grandmother I feel most keenly in Hungarian. *Nagyon szeretlek, Nagymama.* I love you very much, Grandmother. The English sounds formal and disconnected, as though it were located somewhere outside of me, while the Hungarian is inside, nestled in my heart.

My grandmother took pleasure in lyrics sung in languages she didn't understand. The music is what counts, she said, the voice of the singer that matters, not the words at all. But I needed the words, their dictionary-defined security.

I remember one of her many attempts to convince me to appreciate opera as a language of its own, as feeling articulated through pure sound. I was sixteen. It was a rainy afternoon, and I'd returned to Windsor to see her for the weekend. (My parents had moved the family to a different city the previous year, and she was no longer living with us.) When I arrived, she was pounding veal for schnitzel, one of my favourite meals. I sat in the kitchen of her small apartment while she cooked, which was how we always visited, chatting in Hungarian since her English wasn't good, while dinner evolved under her quick and capable hands. She liked to catch up on my latest news: how school was going, how my parents were, was I still seeing "that poet boy" as she referred to my first-ever boyfriend, Jerry, editor of our high school's annual literary journal, friend of drug dealers, and owner of the signet ring I wore, tape-wrapped to fit my finger.

She had the radio tuned, as she regularly did, to a classical station, which at that hour was playing highlights of *Aida*. She enthusiastically extolled the virtues of Verdi and then drifted for a moment into her own memories.

"You need to give opera a chance," she said, smiling. "If only you could go to a performance at the opera house, I'm sure you'd change your mind. In time, in time."

She placed a plate-sized slice of breaded veal into the melted lard. As it sizzled, the room filled with an aroma both enticing and comfortably familiar. I was suddenly hungry. My mother was not at all interested in cooking, so dinner at my grandmother's was always a treat.

"Don't worry," she said. "Someday you'll get there." She, of course, knew what I didn't: that opera required experience, not of music but of life.

I shift in my seat — one of those plush red velvet seats she so vividly described — and I feel her presence more acutely than I have in the nine years since her death. I can't help wondering if perhaps she sat once in the very seat I'm occupying. My throat tightens. If she were here, she'd be like an eager, joyful child waiting for the celebration to begin, hardly able to contain her excitement. I can imagine her voice: "*Hát nem csodálatos?*" *Igen, Nagymama*. It is marvellous, yes.

Usually she launched into her opera stories with: When your *nagypapa* and I saw — here she would fill in the name of the opera she was going to tell me about, then move on to details.

"When your *nagypapa* and I saw *Il Trovatore* for the first time, it was with my brother and his wife, Pista and Rozsa, you remember them?" (I did, but only vaguely and mostly from photographs.) "None of us could figure out the plot, but I didn't care. All I cared about was the music."

Or, on another occasion: "When your *nagypapa* and I went to *Turendot*, it was just the two of us. The tenor who sang the part of Calaf, I can't remember his name of course, but his voice! So full, so majestic! I'm sure I'd recognize it if I heard it today. When he sang 'Nessun Dorma' it sent chills up my spine. *Édesem,* that's one aria you *must* hear!"

And then there was her love of *Madama Butterfly* or, as she called it, *Pillangó Kisasszony.* Of this she had a recording, which she would put on sometimes when, dishes done and espresso poured, we'd play gin rummy at the kitchen table. It was her opinion that this opera contained the most exquisite pieces ever composed for the female voice.

"Listen to that! Just listen!"

I tried to hear what she heard but couldn't, and I was frustrated that I couldn't understand the words. I begged her to let me tune the radio to the local pop station. I remember well those post-dinner evenings. It was surprisingly easy for me to reveal myself to her, for though we disagreed about the value of opera, we agreed about much else, the pleasure of reading especially. And unlike my parents, math majors who grimaced when I announced that I was going to be a writer, my grandmother not only understood my dreams but nourished them.

In those days I was devouring the poetry of e.e.cummings,

the philosophy of Ayn Rand, and as many biographies of artists as I could find. I fantasized endlessly about living a bohemian life, pictured myself drinking *café crème* at Les Deux Magots and writing masterpieces. I had not yet encountered Nin or Durrell or Joyce, nor the dozens of others who waited patiently, their books still undiscovered. The names themselves were poetry: Faulkner, Fitzgerald, Flaubert. Hemingway, Kafka, Kerouac. Proust, Nabokov, Tolstoy. My grandmother did not bat an eye when I announced with arrogant determination that I planned to read my way through the library's entire literature section from A to Z.

I believed that the more I read, the more I would know about life. It didn't occur to me that it could be the other way around: that the more I lived life, the better I would understand what I read.

What did I know at sixteen? That early Beatles songs were fun but *Sergeant Pepper* was art and that Bob Dylan's lyrics were more important than how he sang them. I knew that I was sorry I'd been too young to go to Woodstock. I knew that men had landed on the moon because I'd seen it on television. I knew that although it was 1972, the sixties were not over yet. I knew that literature mattered, but not to most people. Jeans mattered, since my parents had forbidden me to wear them until I started high school. Jerry mattered, but only up to a point, because I had bigger plans than what continuing to date Jerry could possibly include. Grades mattered because they were the means to the next stage of my life, university, for which I already had an intense yearning.

Escape, that was what mattered most. From my parents, from the city they had forced me to live in, from Jerry and his marijuana-induced monologues. Escape was a double direction: what I wanted to escape from, and what I wanted to escape to. That year my best friend Mary gave me a T-shirt as a joke. On the front, in bold black letters: *I came. I saw. I created.* I loved that T-shirt, and it was no joke, at least not to me. I told anyone who was willing to listen that I was moving on, and what I was moving on to was a life of words, a life that mattered.

I'm still not an opera buff, but I've grown to love certain arias, "Nessun Dorma" being one of them. My grandmother would smile knowingly at my choosing *La Bohême* as my first opera in Budapest. She understood how much I longed to be the bohemian I never did become. And although I've not been to Les Deux Magots nor written a masterpiece, I do drink a lot of espresso, and I do write poems. I always order schnitzel when I see it on a menu, and I frequently wear jeans. I'm not fond of Joyce, and I've yet to read Tolstoy or Proust. Rand I discarded long ago, but I still have my *I create* T-shirt, framed and hanging on my study wall. My Beatles and Dylan albums remain in the plastic crate I stored them in when I was sixteen, but since I haven't replaced my old turntable I no longer listen to them. I long ago learned that security is an illusion, in dictionaries or otherwise, and that we don't have to go looking for experience; it will find us soon enough.

If my grandmother were sitting here next to me as the curtain rises, I'd tell her that all is as it should be: I'm living my life, and that is what matters. And now when I listen to music, I don't always need to catch the words.

Tigers Either Way

Not surprisingly, it is while she's out picking strawberries with Kendra that Liz remembers the Zen
parable about the strawberry. It's been years since she
has thought of it, but then it's been years since she and
Kendra picked strawberries, years also since Kendra first
told her the story. They were having lunch in Jordan at Inn
on the Twenty, one of Niagara's first winery restaurants
which had been open only a year. It was the early nine-
ties, sometime in September. The trees had not yet turned,
and it was sunny and warm. Liz can't help smiling at the
memory: the earnestness in Kendra's face as they faced
each other across an enormous bowl of wine-steamed
mussels, Liz's first.

It had been a day of firsts for Liz. It was, for instance,
her first time on Metler Road, the back route Kendra
took on their way to Jordan. Liz had not been aware
of the turkey and chicken farm whose owner kept two
tigers as a living garbage disposal for carcasses that

didn't make the grade. Kendra slowed as they drove past, so Liz could take a good look at the tigers pacing in their enormous cage, and then, several minutes later, stopped at the Comfort Maple, the oldest known sugar maple in the country. Liz loved the name, so suited to the majestic five-hundred-year-old tree. She felt comforted just to be in its presence. She even gave in to her urge to wrap her arms as far around the trunk as they would reach, yet another first. She had certainly not hugged a tree before.

Eventually they arrived in Jordan, parking in front of the Cave Springs Winery. Inn on the Twenty was next to it. The town, the winery, the restaurant — they were all new to Liz, and she was enjoying herself immensely.

It hadn't been Liz's birthday, there was no special occasion at all, but Kendra had insisted on treating her to an outrageously expensive lunch — three full courses, a different wine with each, including a glass of ice wine with dessert. It was a memorable act of friendship. In those days Liz was teaching on contract, which meant that at the end of any given term she might be unemployed. Since her husband had recently been laid off (it was a bad time for middle management), they could hardly pay the hydro bill, never mind dine out. She felt grateful to Kendra but not just for the fine meal. Kendra had inadvertently given her a sense of belonging, finally, to this place, this lush portion of the Niagara peninsula with its vineyards and orchards and cornfields, its slightly hilly roads lined with small farms, its abundance of birds twittering in leafy late-summer trees.

Liz had lived in the area for five years by then, but it wasn't really until that day, exploring the back roads with Kendra, that she had felt at home. The idea of home, elusive and changing, had always been important to her, she whose childhood had been a series of uprootings, nine schools before high school graduation. During lunch, she thought again of the maple she had just seen — imagine, half a millennium in exactly the same spot! Hardly possible, but there it was, living proof, its vast branches extending in various directions like the arms of some Hindu deity. (She has visited the tree many times since that first occasion, still loves to embrace it, stand for long minutes below its wide canopy of leaves. Although she has never mentioned this to anyone, she swears she can feel its life-force.)

During the appetizer, she and Kendra had caught up on general news — which mutual friend was doing what, how Liz's daughter Amy had re-decorated her room — but by the time they got to the main course, a wonderful pan-roasted rosemary salmon, Liz found herself in a long monologue about her stifling marriage, how hard it had become to enjoy life, how difficult it was to see the beauty in the world when the glasses through which it was viewed were caked with mud. (Actually, Liz now remembers, the word she had used was shit. Caked with shit.) It was at that point that Kendra, who had been listening intently, broke in to ask if Liz had ever heard of the Zen strawberry. Liz had not.

"A man crossing a field sees a tiger coming at him, so he starts running. The tiger charges after him, chases him to the edge of a cliff. The guy has no choice but to jump. I mean, hell, there's a tiger coming at him. Anyway, his one chance to save himself is a scrubby branch growing out of the cliff-side halfway down. He grabs the branch and holds on. But when he looks down, guess what he sees? Another tiger! Then he notices that close by, just within his reach, there's a small plant growing from the rock, and one ripe strawberry hanging from it. It's intensely red, the most beautiful berry he's ever seen. He stretches out his arm as far as he can and gets it. But don't forget: there's still a tiger above and a tiger below."

"Sounds like a caught-between-a rock-and-a-hard-place scenario. Too bad the guy can't fly."

"Exactly. A bird wouldn't have this problem. But for him, there's no escape. So he stays focused on the berry. He reaches out, and picks it, and when he brings it to his lips, it tastes sweeter than anything he's ever tasted."

"So how does the story end?"

"The same way all life stories end. He dies."

The strawberry field is large and green, the berries a vivid startling red. Many are hidden, so you have to part the leaves, then tug slightly to get each berry from the stem. Picking is a deliberate, conscious act. Liz remembers reading somewhere, probably some women's magazine with recipes, that strawberries are the only fruit that carry their seeds on the outside — approximately two hundred per berry. That's some reproductive system, she thinks, as she gently plucks one, pops it into her mouth. It's delicious, sweet and warm from the sun.

Liz glances at Kendra, several rows over. She is a short woman, a good six inches shorter than Liz who stands five-eight in bare feet. Her bent form, straight shoulder-length brown hair held back with a clip, is silhouetted against the green rows and the blue sky. She is dressed in baggy denim shorts and a pale yellow T-shirt, arms and legs tanned and solid. She is a woman who inhabits her body without apology or embarrassment. Liz has always felt that there was something calming about Kendra. A sense of consistency, an unshakeable trust that if you just lived in the moment, the future would take care of itself.

Funny though, how life goes. Now, a decade after that memorable Jordan lunch, it is Kendra who worries about the bills, has the pre-school children, the stifling marriage, the unappreciative husband. It is now she who stays at home, who cannot afford to go out, who no longer buys books and CDs or travels to foreign countries. Recently, when Roy's car gave out, her freedom was curtailed even further. They can't afford a new vehicle, so Roy now takes hers. It's almost impossible to imagine Kendra, who loves to drive, without wheels. It's like imagining a bird without wings. How, Liz wonders, can she stand it?

The shift has been happening gradually and began with Liz's divorce and Kendra's marriage, both of which occurred in the same year: 2000. Roy is no match for Kendra, and if he were abusive, Liz is certain Kendra would have left him by now. But he hasn't been; he has just remained immature and disengaged, an unformed being, blandly neutral. His greatest asset, as far as Liz can see, is that he is easy to control — or, to put it another way, he's "malleable." Kendra can call most of the shots mainly because of Roy's indifference to anything even remotely domestic, including his wife and children. What Roy cares about is his job at the golf club (seasonal, so he's unemployed every winter), his weekly beer night with the boys, and his relentless TV watching. And his sleep, of course. Roy cares about his sleep. If the baby cries, Kendra can deal with it.

Kendra, not so long ago, after a few glasses of wine during a rare childless evening over at Liz's, did admit that life with Roy had its limitations. "He keeps me and the kids on a shelf. He looks at us once in a while, likes to know we're there, even admires us at times. Occasionally, he takes us down to show us off. To his parents, friends, whoever we should be shown off to. And then he puts us back on the shelf."

Liz remembers how often Kendra used to laugh, a delightful spontaneous belly laugh with which she celebrated the world. When Kendra laughed, you had to laugh with her. Her laughter never failed to make Liz feel better, even when she was the most down. But Kendra was a lot less joyful these days, and there was a resigned air about her.

Liz thinks back again to that extravagant lunch, to Kendra's patience and kindness and generosity, which should have guaranteed her karmic immunity from the likes of Roy. Liz's own marital episode, of twelve years' duration, had ended in an acrimonious divorce, Scott threatening to cut the kitchen table in half as part of the equal division of property. He had given her a much harder time than any of her friends or relatives could have guessed but she, like Kendra, had kept her problems to herself. It was too embarrassing to admit you had married a jerk because what did that make *you*.

Liz knew that jumping to conclusions about other people's relationships was not only futile but unfair — dangerous even. There were always two sides, and there was always more to the story than even the participants realized. Liz knew all the clichés. Yet she couldn't help resenting Roy, his self-centredness, his irresponsible habits, his unappreciative treatment of Kendra. Lately she had begun entertaining fantasies of telling him off, which of course she wouldn't do. But she wondered why Kendra didn't.

Liz was puzzled by this unexpected compliance in Kendra who seemed to have surrendered herself to an unhealthy situation with disturbing complacency. Maybe this had something to do with having small children, with not rocking the boat, with holding the ladder steady. How many wives had stuck with unsuitable husbands for decades for this very reason? How many, like Kendra, had created a life within a life? Roy was part of the outside layer while she and the kids operated on the inside.

It was an unusually hot June morning, and getting hotter. Liz breathed in the sweet smell of the sun-warmed berries. Her eyes felt tired from squinting. She should have been smart like Kendra and brought her sunglasses. There was no breeze either, the air hanging heavy and motionless. She wasn't used to so much bending and squatting, felt slightly dizzy if she stood up too suddenly. The heat reminded her of the one vacation she and Scott had ever taken, to Mexico, when she had keeled over in the heat at some Mayan ruin she could no longer even remember. But she could remember Scott's cold reaction, and how he had acted as if she'd fainted on purpose, for attention. And she could remember her intense dislike for him, blossoming out from that moment, and how she could not ever root it out again.

She didn't often contemplate Scott these days because, fortunately, she didn't have to. He had moved to Vancouver after the divorce, opting to stay in touch with his daughter only at Christmas and on her birthday. Not much of a family man, Scott. And yet Liz had stayed with him, stayed long after she had admitted, though only to herself, that she no longer loved him. That, in fact, marrying him had been a mistake. Stayed because of Amy, because of money, because of habit, because somehow, at that moment, it seemed to be the safest thing to do. Staying, leaving. Tigers either way.

Liz looks over again at Kendra, who wears a broad smile. Kendra stretches, raising her arms high above her head. "Pretty good picking today! God, these berries are incredible, aren't they?"

Liz returns the grin. "Yeah, they sure are." As Kendra once said to her: "Lovers come and go, but friends remain." As she picks up her full basket, she makes a silent wish for Kendra's happiness. What a splendid sight it would be, to watch a bird pluck a strawberry from the cliff-side, and without the slightest fear of tigers, soar away.

Ecstasy

Wine brings to light the hidden secrets of the soul....
—Horace

"Hi there." I look up from the tasting menu. "Sorry to keep you waiting. Which wines will you be trying today?" The voice is friendly, low and melodic. It belongs to an attractive woman, thirtyish, who stands in front of me behind the large horseshoe-shaped bar. Since I, too, am standing and we're both tall, we're face to face. Her eyes are startling, green with a hint of yellow, like a cat's.

"I think I'll try just the cabernet sauvignon and the merlot, thanks."

She's slim, the word *lithe* comes to mind, and wears the staff uniform well: black pants, crisp white blouse open at the collar, loose black tie. Pours the wines gracefully. On her right ring finger, an oval moonstone set in silver, the only jewellery. Her straight black hair is chin-length, falls forward when she looks down. Her nameplate says *Cynthia*.

I take a healthy sip of the cab sauve. Roll it around on

my tongue before swallowing. Although I love the poetry of wine terms — earthy, elegant, robust — I'm not much good at applying them, at least not to wines.

Cynthia considers me. "Are you Laurel by any chance?"

"Yes, I am." She's caught me off guard.

"My uncle mentioned you were coming."

"He's letting me use one of the guest houses for the weekend. Very generous of him. Is he around? I'd like to thank him."

I take a sip of the merlot.

"No, he's away in California on business. Won't be back 'til next week. He thinks you're terrific by the way. You know that article you wrote about him, that one in *Urban Living* last year? He's got it framed in his office. He keeps telling people that it put him and the winery on the map. His words."

She smiles, nods toward the now empty glasses. The eyes really are striking. They look as though they might belong to some powerful female divinity. And the way she moves, so at ease in her body, reminds me of Angel. But I don't want to think about that.

"So which do you like best?"

"The cab sauve."

"I like that one too. Here, take a bottle with you. On the house. I'm sure my uncle would insist." She smiles again. I don't tell her that today is my thirty-first birthday.

A large tour group tromps in, blinking as their eyes adjust. Some of them head directly toward the shelves of Riedel glasses on display, others toward the row of specialty food items. One woman exclaims loudly enough for the entire room to hear: "Oh, how wonderful! Ice wine truffles!" The wine aficionados head directly for the tasting bar.

"I'd better be going. Looks like you've got company. Thanks for the samples."

"Come and try the whites later."

I don't go back. I avoid the fancy restaurant on the premises for dinner, too; opt instead to drive into Woodsville, five minutes down the road. For a town of five thousand, it has a surprisingly sophisticated grocery store. I pick up a baguette and two croissants, some old white cheddar and smoked Gouda, a large hunk of Stilton, an extra-large bar of dark chocolate, seedless grapes, coffee — and, as a birthday treat, a delightfully over-sized éclair. Plenty to get me through to Sunday. Since the guest house has a kitchenette, I won't have to eat alone in public, which is a relief. If there's one thing I don't like, it's dining by myself. And I wouldn't be if things had worked out differently. If Angel had joined me as she had said she might. She took off to Vegas with friends instead. So much for planning. Or should I say *my* planning. Then again, maybe it's best to leave certain lusts unrequited.

I tune the radio to a classical music station, open the complimentary bottle of cab sauve, prop myself comfortably on the queen-size bed. My blank notebook and

decade-old copy of *The Alexandria Quartet* (*Justine,
Balthazar, Mountolive* and *Clea* — all in one volume)
are waiting. Also a massive history of wine, the cabin's
only book-in-residence. I've been planning to re-read
the *Quartet* ever since I was reminded of it by an article
about Durrell in *The Globe* last year, but have been too
busy. I'm into the last chapter of *Justine* now, though it's
taken me several weeks to get this far. At least out here in
wine country I might get more than a dozen pages read
at a time. The notebook is simply habit, or maybe my
version of a security blanket. I can't seem to go anywhere
without it.

I close Durrell and switch to the wine history. I'm intrigued by the chapter on the Mysteries of Dionysus, the
ancient Greek women's festival. An early version of girls'
night out. Once a year the men allowed the women to
leave their homes, go into the forest and let off steam. It
was their one chance to connect as a group, share their
stories. Attendance was optional, but I bet no one ever
declined. The secret rituals went unrecorded, but myth
has it that there was a lot of barbaric behaviour. The
nursing of wild animals, copious wine consumption,
frenzied dancing, fierce female sex. Even hunting. The
girls showed they could do a lot more than gather berries and bake bread. Apparently, there was no shortage
of ecstasy.

Ecstasy. The word lingers, as I read on.

The festival was not popular with the guys mostly
because they had no control over it. Many would have

undoubtedly enjoyed it as a spectator sport even if they weren't allowed to participate, but they weren't permitted anywhere near it. They let their wives and daughters go only because it was safer in the long run than not to. Imagine all that pent-up female energy with no release, not even once a year!

It gives me an odd little jolt, when I come across the name Cynthia. I didn't realize the name was Greek. I can't help but think of Jim Hewitt's niece, Cynthia of the Tasting Bar. The resident goddess of the winery. I wonder how she's spending her Friday night, where she lives, what she does when she's not working for her uncle. What we might talk about if she were here. I wonder right to the end of one glass of wine and into the next. And she does look uncannily like Angel.

After a while, I start reading *Balthazar* and realize that I don't like Durrell quite as well as I did the first time I read him, when I was twenty. He doesn't seem to understand his female characters although he pretends to. He does have some fine passages though. This one ends up in my notebook: *We live lives based upon selected fictions. Our view of reality is conditioned by our position in space and time — not by our personalities as we like to think. Thus every interpretation of reality is based upon a unique position. Two paces east or west and the whole picture is changed.*

Michael and I have now been apart for five months. When he moved out, I was suddenly cut loose from the life I had been living for eight years. I careened unhooked, unhanded, like a kite whose owner has let go of the string. It didn't make it any easier that it was at my own request. After a year of vacillation, I'd finally screwed up the nerve to tell him I couldn't continue. He wanted to know why, of course, and although I'd practised dozens of speeches to answer that very question, they failed me. All I could say was I couldn't stay in a relationship where laundry was more important than art. He said that was a pretty lame answer, and he was right. But I didn't have the guts to put words to the truth: I had found myself attracted to a co-worker named Angel, part of whose attraction was that she seemed to be anything but angelic.

My marriage to Michael was never what you would call wildly happy, but the beginning was certainly happier than the end. At least at the beginning we had a coupled life. He was my first truly serious relationship, and I have since thought many times that this was part of the problem. I naively thought that my first real love affair should also be my last.

I did love him in those early days — or thought I did. We spent a lot of time together, talked about more than whose turn it was to clean the bathroom. We did things in the world. We went out to dinner, bars, concerts, plays, art exhibits. We took an interest in each other's work. We even read some of the same books. We found auctions, got great deals on old furniture which we then refinished. We visited family, hung out with friends. We had pleasant sex, regularly. What was lacking, though I would have argued in those days that it wasn't, was intimacy. Real closeness. The kind where both people feel authentic, equal, and safe. The kind I had with my female friends.

Somewhere along the line Michael's and my relationship changed, or more accurately *we* changed. We became a marital cliché. He got two promotions within one year, started working longer hours, stopped reading. I was working less but sleeping more, both of which he resented. Sex became a fight word. Eventually, *every* word became a fight word.

It got worse. My job as a writer for *Urban Living* had always been stressful, but at least it had been exciting. Fun, even. I'd always looked forward to the next interview, the next article, even if it was about the latest shoe boutique opening in Yorkville. But this changed too. I grew intensely bored, a foreign state for me. I wanted to write something *meaningful,* but the only meaningful things I wrote were the quotes from others that I collected in my notebook. There were many from Anaïs Nin in those days. *We don't see things as they are, we see things as we are.* And: *Life is a process of becoming, a combination of states we have to go through. Where people fail is that they wish to elect a state and remain in it. This is a kind of death.* And: *Life shrinks or expands according to one's courage.* Her words mattered, and I wanted to have conversations with Michael that mattered. I was tired of talking about the weather.

My boredom began as a mild lethargy, a general lack-lustre attitude, which was at first easy to ignore. Gradually though, it expanded into an overwhelming desire for unconsciousness. It was more severe than just sleeping in on weekends. I was now often asleep by eight. Sometimes I woke up in the morning knowing that I had dreamt, but couldn't remember what.

I began to yearn for enchantment and remembered fondly the delightful insurrections of my childhood: subversive mouthfuls of snow, the finger in the whipped cream when no one was looking. Spontaneity. Laughter. The healing power of foolishness.

My discontent was finally and irrevocably triggered one Monday morning. The starter gun, whose sound I suddenly realized I had been braced for, exploded and I was off and running. Michael was driving me to work, which he did occasionally when he was in the mood. We were stopped at the corner of Bay and Bloor in rush-hour traffic. I looked around at the hordes: pedestrians, fellow drivers, passengers. I thought of the people in office buildings, ascending elevators, arriving at desks. The apartment dwellers blow-drying their hair, drinking coffee in quick gulps, one eye on the clock, always. I thought of all the other people in the world at that very moment, all of us in simultaneous existence, each of us occupying our own miniscule space at the same time. Billions of human beings in the present. Breathing, now.

And then it hit me: eventually, without exception, every person alive at this moment would one day not be. The entire population of the entire world would be gone. One by one at various points, we would all vacate our spaces. *I will one day be dead. Everyone on my street will be dead. Everyone in my city will be dead. Everyone in my province, in my country, on my continent, will be dead. Everyone on the planet will be absolutely, uncontrollably dead.* These were the actual words that went through my mind as I sat there watching the light change. I tried to tell Michael how I was feeling. He looked at me with undisguised condescension. "You're weird, you know that?" He pushed down hard on the gas. My stomach lurched as we shot through the intersection.

I knew at that point that lacklustre just wouldn't cut it any more, nor would escaping into sleep. And once you know something, you can't un-know it. I had to move in a different direction, away from Michael. Given my tendency to procrastinate, however, this movement might have taken a long time. But as it happened, Angel started as an editorial assistant for *Urban Living* on that very day. I felt my first pangs of unrequited lust. I also started sleeping less but dreaming more. And what I dreamt about was Angel.

On Saturday, I take a tour of the winery. Learn about *terroir* and *vitis vinifera*, tannins and acidity. Learn about aging and complexity and balance. Life lessons. Learn that the roses planted at the ends of the vine rows aren't mere decoration but warning signals, like canaries in mines. Rose bushes are sensitive to some of the same things vines are sensitive to — black rot, bugs. If the roses suffer, it's time for preventative measures. It means the vines will be next. If only marriages came with rose bushes, Michael and I would at least have been warned. Then again, no warning would have been enough to counteract Angel.

I skip the tasting session at the end of the tour, go for a hike instead. It feels good, the rhythm of moving, one foot after the other touching ground, lifting off again. I walk for a long time through the acres of vineyards, row upon row of lush, grape-heavy vines, their renegade tendrils shooting skyward. If longing has a colour, it is green, this light-dappled summer green that stretches to the vanishing point.

Finally, I give in to temptation and return to the tasting room. She's there, talking with a pair of young couples who are on a bike tour together. She sees me come in. Her cat eyes flicker. "Hi, Laurel."

"Hi," I say, then walk to the far end of the room, take four bottles of cabernet sauvignon from the shelf, pay the cashier, and flee.

It is now well past sunset. The birds are asleep, but the crickets blanket the dark landscape with sound. I pour another glass of wine, stand sipping it at the open kitchen window. The solstice moon hangs over the horizon, perfectly round and much larger than usual. It illuminates the vine rows, which run like tracks into the night. I will be leaving early tomorrow, want to miss the Sunday traffic heading back to Toronto. I don't know yet whether I will go back to the tasting room. If I do, perhaps Cynthia will have her back to me when I enter. Perhaps, if I take just one or two paces toward her, she will turn.

Hemingway and the Buddha

"So how's the fruit today?" Randall swears by fresh fruit.

"It's good."

"Did you see any guava?"

"No, just pineapples. Bananas." Meg finds it hard to get excited about fruit, fresh or otherwise.

"What about those wonderful tomatoes we had yesterday?"

"I didn't see any"

"Too bad."

They were almost late for breakfast, served only until ten, so headed quickly in separate directions to fill up their plates — it's a large dining hall with various buffet stations throughout — and then met at the corner table they've occupied during every meal since they arrived three days ago. Randall doesn't like crowds especially while he's eating. He prefers to be as far away from their fellow diners as possible. This is why, despite the fact that Meg prefers noise, the steady dish clatter and conversational hum around her, they sit at the far end of the room.

"They'll probably have more tomatoes tomorrow."

"You know, Meg —"

"What?"

"There really isn't anyone to blame."

"I'm not blaming anyone for the lack of tomatoes."

"Come on, you know that's not what I meant."

"Yes, there *is* someone to blame, Randall. *You.*"

He takes a slow sip of coffee, tries to keep his voice even. "I'm not set on anything. I haven't accepted the position yet. We haven't put our house up for sale. I'm just trying to have a discussion with you."

"You could've told me about your promotion before we came. Or you could've waited until we got home. This is supposed to be our vacation. You've ruined it."

"You're being melodramatic."

"Whatever."

"Can't we talk about this?"

"Talk about what exactly? About everything we'd be leaving behind? How about a discussion about *my* job? Our friends? We agreed when we got married that we'd stay in St. Catharines, that we both liked it there."

"But, Meg, things change. You know that. This is an incredible opportunity, not just for me. For us. It would mean a lot more money. You wouldn't have to work at all if you didn't feel like it."

"But I do feel like it. I've always felt like it."

"Let's not talk about it right now."

"Yes, let's not. I'm going down to the beach."

"I thought you were hungry."

"Well, you were wrong."

Meg isn't keen on all-inclusive resorts, but the price was right and a week in Cuba, where there would be no American tourists, had seemed like a fine idea. She was more than ready for a vacation, and so far the Sol Cayo Santa Maria has proved to be acceptably pleasant. Clean, spacious, uncluttered, with plenty of palm and *caleta* trees, hibiscus and bougainvillea. The buildings and vegetation well-balanced, neither dominating the other. The staff courteous and friendly but not overbearing.

To get to the beach, hotel guests must pass three immaculate swimming pools rimmed with blue-and-white-striped lounge chairs. The loudspeakers are thumping non-stop as usual. This morning a loud male voice blares over the *merengue*, exhorting pool-loungers to get up and dance. Meg is relieved when she is finally out of the noise and her feet touch sand. The tropical charisma of the white-sand beach is undeniable. Small shells, some worn to a perfect smoothness, shine like porcelain in the sun, and she stoops now and again to gather some. There is the occasional cigarette butt or plastic cocktail straw or clump of dried seaweed, but the debris is raked under each morning, so the beach appears remarkably clean.

Meg finds a spot that is still deserted though she knows this won't last long, not once breakfast ends. She spreads her beach towel on the white plastic chaise, near a *cabana* in case she wants shade later. There is no sign of Randall yet, but she knows he will soon join her. He is slow to anger and doesn't hold a grudge. In this she can trust. It is she who tends to flare and keep burning.

She opens *The Collected Stories of Ernest Hemingway*. It's the Finca Vigia edition, a hefty paperback. She figured it would be fun reading it in Cuba, but with each story she has finished, she's become more irritated. Hemingway's despair is overwhelming. She wants to feel sorry for him, for the hollowness he found at the heart of everything, but his misogyny and posturing are off-putting. Nothing was ever quite good enough or beautiful enough. Nothing could last. Nothing could hide what was, at heart, his own gaping neediness.

After a while, Meg closes the book. It feels good to sit back and do nothing but face the sky and the ocean. She finds it odd that they don't quite match, like two different landscapes that have been spliced together, top and bottom incongruous. The sky is much like the southern Ontario blue of home, not too light, not too dark, with clouds that remind her of freshly fluffed white pillows. But the ocean, the ocean is entirely different from anything she's ever seen. It is compelling eye music performed in variations, bands of turquoise, teal, medleys of blue and green, crescendoing into a dark inky line at the horizon. She's always thought that water reflects sky, yet this water doesn't seem to reflect the sky at all, but is entirely unto itself, perfect.

She watches Randall approach in his tidy black bathing suit that looks more like a pair of shorts. A thirty-four-year-old investment banker with short-cropped hair, already receding. Good legs. The beginning of middle-age spread offset by height and broad shoulders and a confident posture. Sometimes she wonders if that's all that attracted her to him in the first place, his tall male confidence. He's holding drinks, a *cerveza* for him, a lime daiquiri for her. She thinks her conspicuous consumption of daiquiris must be due to the Hemingway influence. He drank his sugarless, as does she.

Randall removes his sunglasses. He always worries that they'll give him raccoon eyes if he leaves them on too long. He takes his tanning, like everything else, seriously.

"So how are you feeling?" he says.

"Fine."

He sighs, and opts for silence as the safest course.

Meg stares out at the ocean and finds herself focusing on a pelican performing nose-dives. It's a large, impressive bird, almost a metre long, with brown plumage except for its white belly and the white stripe on the underside of its wings. It flies low over the water, scouting fish. When it spots its prey, it turns abruptly and dives straight down, collapsing its wings like a bellows at the last instant before plunging headfirst into the water. Then it surfaces, drains the water from its bill, tips its head back, swallows its catch. Meg watches intently, without blinking.

A couple, holding hands, walks past directly in Meg's line of vision. She's wearing a flamingo-pink bikini, he an aqua thong, neon against sun-darkened skin. He's a lot taller than she is, and they look as though they frequent a gym. Probably have exotic names like Sven and Marielle or Lars and Ursula. Meg suspects though that if she saw them up close they'd turn out to be older than they look from this distance. She shifts her attention for a moment to Randall. The pink backside has caught his eye though he's trying hard not to turn his head. Meg stares at Sven. She hopes that Randall will notice.

A group of Italian couples has settled nearby. Meg watches them go hesitantly into the water, then with increasing exuberance. Once again the beach flag is red as it has been every day. There's a steady wind, and the waves are high and continuous. Those who surrender, who let the wave move them, who rise with it, are delivered to the shore. Those who try to fight it are swept under, gasp for air as they surface. Meg doesn't feel like going into the water at all. Randall rolls over onto his stomach. She watches him as she watched the pelican.

The sun climbs higher. Meg can hear the rustle of the palm trees, their sharp foliage like feathers made of blades. Randall heaves himself up, announces that he's getting more beer.

"Do you want another daiquiri?"

"Sure," she says. "Why not?"

Two older women — Meg guesses they're in their sixties — have settled in under the *cabana*. One is sheltered by a flamboyant straw hat, the other sports a bandana. They're speaking English. Bandana is reading what must be a book about Buddhism. She talks about Buddha's mother having dreamt of a white elephant before his birth, says something about elephants and knowledge which Meg isn't quite able to catch. But she does manage to hear what comes next, a passage about two hens who don't know that they're about to be slaughtered. One hen tells the other that the rice is much tastier than the corn, that the corn is slightly off. "The hen is talking about relative joy," Bandana reads. "She does not realize that the real joy of the moment is the joy of not being slaughtered, the joy of being alive."

Meg would like to hear what Straw Hat says to this, but Randall has returned and is making a big deal of how difficult it is to carry drinks and snacks at once.

"Next time, I'll go," she says.

"It's all right. I'm not complaining."

He drinks his beer in one long swallow. "It's getting pretty hot out here," he says.

"Yes, it is."

Give me non-anger, non-ignorance, non-regret, non-pain. She knows even as she silently wishes for these things that you can take them all away and not necessarily end up with their opposites. Randall isn't a bad man. She's not a bad woman. Their four-year marriage hasn't been a bad marriage. As she slowly finishes her daiquiri, she thinks of Randall in their room that morning, beach towel in hand, admiring her collection of shells. His concentration as he picked them up one by one, turned them over, examined them with genuine interest before replacing them gently to the exact spot where she had originally set them.

"Time to get out of the sun," he says. "You're going to burn."

"Yes."

Everything is a matter of degree, she thinks. How badly you burn, what you settle for, what you're willing to give up. She gathers up her towel and the empty glasses. Hemingway she leaves in the sand.

Horoscopes

... no love can survive muteness.
—Milan Kundera

I can see now how the end began: you spent February 14 out for dinner with friends, arrived the following week bearing daffodils. You said you didn't believe in Valentine's Day, but you would humour me.

It is now August. I'm thankful, as I sit here with my second glass of wine on this Queenston Heights patio, that your city is far away across the lake. I'm thankful that I can barely see the gray outline of its downtown buildings, the CN Tower so small it looks like a toy. And I'm thankful for the distance between us. It ensures that I won't run into you at the supermarket or anywhere else in my daily life. My real life, I almost said.

I'm through with trying to understand who you are or what you want. We've dragged things out for months. As the Niagara River continues into Lake Ontario so, too, have we continued. Nature taking its course. But even rivers end. Some flow into lakes; others just dry up.

Toronto. It seems like a mirage, as unreachable as you are in your bachelor apartment with its espresso machine and glass dining-room table. Today, charismatic charlatan, my eyes are powerful. They can see through your walls.

There you are — legs crossed, hands behind your head, laid out on the black leather couch, staring at your prized aquarium in perfect silence. The fish glide back and forth in the water, go nowhere. There is a thin layer of dust on the solitary bookshelf which contains your random books, most of them given to you by others. There is a phone beside you, and it rings. You check the call display. It is Catherine, so of course you answer it.

This wine is good. Very good. A Peller cabernet sauvignon. I'm immensely glad you're not here drinking it with me.

From this height, the river has an odd weave of currents, looks almost frozen, stopped in time. You have to look really closely to see it move, and even then the movement is almost imperceptible. Not unlike life, really, if you think about it. Not that you would.

The large chestnut tree that hangs partially over the patio was here long before the restaurant was, and there's a sweet summer stillness in the air. A few tables over, a couple enjoys a late lunch. He looks like a jovial, well-adjusted type. Big smile for his dining companion — I'm assuming it's his wife — when she puts her hand over his. I can picture you smirking. Sentimental gestures are not your style. In the far corner, a man in a white open-collared golf shirt, sixty-ish, nurses a pint of beer. Spared the usual horde of tourists, we are the only ones here on this quiet Wednesday, beneath a miniature General Brock who towers over us from the tall column of his monument. He is too high up to be distinguished. He could be anyone. Distance, the great equalizer. From this far away, you too could be anyone. I find this notion oddly comforting. I'm tired of talking to you in my head, but I can't seem to stop. There are things I need to say, even if you are unwilling to hear them. I'm also tired of resorting to horoscopes but read them anyway. Someone left a stack of newspapers on the next table. When I first sat down, I couldn't resist flipping to the horoscope pages.

One advised:

> *Mars is providing the power, and Venus is bestowing the opportunity for you to do something that is important to your future. But you need to summon the clarity and conviction to make it all work. Reach for it. You will find it.*

Another:

> *Even though you are ready to make changes, you are hesitant. To achieve your full potential, you must act. Do not shy away from making decisions — or mistakes.*

The third:

Enjoy life. Write your own ticket. Take chances, diversify.

I'm choosing the last one. My next glass of cab merlot will be from Henry of Pelham, not Vineland Estates. Diversification. We never did get out to the Vineland winery although we talked about going several times. The one time we almost made it there, we ended up in bed instead. You looked at me with such focus that I felt as though no one had ever quite seen me before. *You're so beautiful.* The words tumbled from your mouth easily in those days, and I was eager to believe them.

On the facing page, there's a strange headline: "Words Affect Water." The opening paragraph:

Japanese scientist Masaru Emoto has made a worldwide splash with his experiments featuring the effects of verbal messages on water. Dr. Emoto put signs on bottles of water. Some of these signs were positive, such as "Thank You" and "Love and Gratitude." Others were negative, such as "You Fool" and "You Make Me Sick, I Will Kill You." He has published several books featuring remarkable photographs showing frozen water crystals affected by these verbal messages. The water with the positive messages formed beautiful crystals; the water with the negative messages

*became ugly and malformed. Dr. Emoto has com-
mented that since our bodies are composed mostly
of water, it could be concluded that such messages
would have a profound effect on us as well.*

Words do have an effect, and I'm aware that while
yours have gotten fewer and falser, mine have become
charged with anger and have multiplied at an alarming
rate. I don't like the me who has recently shown up.

You continue to insist that your feelings for me haven't
changed. You say you are just intensely busy, and that is
why it's best if I don't drive up to see you. It occurs to me
with increasing frequency that you're lying about your
busy-ness. I can't help but wonder what else you've lied
about or simply omitted mentioning. No wonder you
hate questions. Every time you're asked one, you're faced
with a choice: to tell the truth or to lie. You don't like the
black-and-white aspect of this. It leaves you no room to
manoeuvre, and manoeuvre is what you do best.

Hard to know what's really going on since you refuse
to discuss anything that might throw you into a negative
light. You want everyone, including my friends, to like
you. You like being liked. It makes you feel good about
yourself when people tell you how funny you are, how
sociable. When I try to discuss your life in Toronto, the
boundaries you're crossing with Catherine, you accuse
me of being jealous. A convenient word, "jealous." It
lets you off the hook. You don't have to look at anything
you're doing.

When I get upset, you suddenly need "space." You don't argue. It would be too messy, and you don't like your women to be too emotional. Feelings tend to complicate things. Leaving is your preferred option. You strut your indifference, wave your false bravado like a red cape, then escape to your car, speed away, back to the fish and the leather couch.

In my mind, a classic snapshot of you: the back of your black Mustang as you full-throttle it down the street. Magnificently.

And then, of course, there is the most memorable scene of all: your absence in the seat beside me as the plane took off toward Arizona in the livid dusk. The seat was royal blue. I stared at it for many long hours, will never forget the exact shade.

It might almost be entertaining, your ongoing monologue about Catherine, if you hadn't lived with her before I happened onto the scene. You always speak of her in the present tense, which makes me speculate about how much of an ex she really is. Catherine leaves the building when there is an argument. Catherine flirts with whoever is available and then denies she was flirting. Catherine smokes pot in front of her kids. Catherine treats her dogs better than her friends. Catherine boasts that she is a gourmet cook, but she never cooks anything. Catherine likes to have everyone around her wait on her hand and foot. Catherine leaves dirty dishes in the sink for days. Catherine once greeted one of your friends topless just for the fun of seeing both of your faces. Catherine spends too much money on clothes. Catherine's got too much corporate attitude. Catherine pretends to know everything about everything. Catherine lacks class, but she gets promotions anyway. Catherine, Catherine, Catherine. I have grown to hate the name, a name I used to love. My favourite girl's name since adolescence when I first read *Wuthering Heights*. A name I considered giving to a daughter, if I ever had one. A name now ruined.

I suspect that even if I left the picture, Catherine would still be in it. You will always need your extra-curricular activities.

You have set it up amazingly well: have kept both of us caught in your net, competing against each other, with you as star at the centre of the colluding universe. I wonder how you play her, what it is she knows, doesn't know. How you work me into the conversation or leave me out, depending on what is called for, what is expedient at the time.

The Arizona fiasco should have finished us, but I guess I wasn't ready yet. Needed to learn a few more lessons the hard way. I was a bad case. What kind of masochist would continue a relationship with someone who stands her up at the airport? At the end of February we'd booked a one-week holiday to the American Southwest, where neither of us had been. It seemed like a good idea, an adventure. A chance for us to spend more than a weekend together.

Two weeks before our May first departure, you decided that we should call the whole thing off. Forfeit the tickets. You developed an acute case of money shortage, claimed you couldn't afford to go. I said I would pay for the hotel and meals. Ordinarily, you would have jumped at such an offer. And then the truth appeared. Catherine had threatened never to speak to you again if you went. Worse, she threatened to follow us down there. Why, I wondered, had you told her where we were going? The name of the hotel, even? I continued to beg you not to cancel the trip. You kept vacillating, said you wanted to go, but....

Finally the day arrived. I sat in the departure lounge, stunned with disbelief. Fifteen minutes before boarding, and still no sign of you. I dialled your number. It astounds me even now, almost four months later, that you had the gall to pick up the phone.

In what surely must've been the understatement of the year, I observed: *I take it you're not coming.* And then, in a tone I hoped was steely enough to knife into the heart of your silence, I told you that I was now going to get on the plane and didn't want to speak to you again. Ever.

I hit END on the cell phone. Unfortunately, it wasn't. Like a piranha whose meal got away, you realized you'd lost something you weren't done with yet, and so, buoyed by your mother's zero-balance VISA card (which you borrowed since yours, as usual, was at its limit) you raced to Arizona. You made it in forty-eight hours. I felt stupidly sorry for you when you arrived, hungry and exhausted, on the verge, just barely, of contrition. What I also felt, I'm embarrassed to admit, was undeniable lust. It was something you counted on, this lust. You expected that I would let you into my room, and I did.

A friend recently advised: *If you're ecstatic, great; otherwise, cut your losses.* If only losses could be trimmed as if they were loose threads hanging from sleeves or hair in need of shaping. But losses aren't tangible like delicate cat whiskers or the brittle ribs of autumn leaves. If they were, they'd be thick cords of hemp knotted and re-knotted, and it would be Fate wielding the scissors. Ah, there I go again, lapsing into poetry. I know you hate it when I do that. And just for the record: I'm no longer ecstatic.

I love you, you would say during those early weeks when it was still convenient, when like a manipulative child you wanted something. Help with your résumé, free dinners accompanied by expensive wines, sex, my total attention. I now understand why you said you preferred older women. Sometimes the seven years between us felt like seventeen.

I love you. After a while, I couldn't hear the words without wincing. When you stopped saying them altogether, at least I knew you were finally telling a version of the truth. *Love is a behaviour*, I said to you once. I remember how quizzically you looked at me. Love, for you, has never been about behaviour. Never about actions matching words. Love, for you, is an idea, exciting and entertaining while it lasts, which isn't long. Inadvertently you taught me not what love is, but what it is not. A useful lesson, in the long run.

I wonder if you even remember our most recent phone conversation. It was just last Thursday, and I can recall it exactly.

"So, have you seen Catherine lately?"

Silence.

"Didn't you say she called last week?"

Silence.

"What did she want anyway?"

Silence.

"Did you have dinner with her?"

Silence.

"Why do you keep seeing someone whose house you moved out of because you couldn't stand her?"

Silence.

"Don't you think this is weird? You tell me how awful she is and then go running off to be with her every time she calls?"

Silence.

"Why do you keep dragging your past into our present?"

Silence.

"So are you coming down this weekend?"

"I'll have to see."

"What do you have to see?"

"How much work I have to do."

"Bring some of it down here with you. I'll make us dinner."

"It's better if I work here."

"Better?"

"It's better for me."

"I'm sure it is."

Silence.

The couple have become aware of my presence. They're just finishing their meal, have asked for the bill. She looks over with what might be sympathy; he's just plain curious. This is as good a time as any for me to order another glass of wine. When it arrives, Golf Shirt will probably raise his pint to me and wink. That's what he did the last time.

Fortunately, projections have a limited screen life. They fade as realities shift into focus, as facts impose themselves. You would like me to tell you that I'll never love again. That you have been the most important one, the truly Significant Other. Of course we all need to think that each love is the grand love, the ultimate love. How could we love otherwise? This might come as a surprise to you: what I felt for you was never love, though it has taken me far too long to recognize this. I succumbed to the ego boost of your attention. I felt attractive because you said I was. I became, temporarily, a lovely crystal because of your words. And then, as your words changed, so did I.

Here's the strangest thing: you and I will both be dead someday. Inevitably, Fate will arrive, clear-eyed and adamant, scissors in hand. Will announce, matter-of-factly: here I am, deal with it. In the meantime, this is what I have learned: that I have to end our relationship. That I need to stop blaming you for the fact that I didn't end it sooner. That although I'm still angry, it is mostly at myself, and it is within my power to stop the anger. That if I give myself the right words, I can create my own horoscope: *choose, forgive, grow.*

Glacial Erratic

We were both in a mood, Jack and I, as we said goodbye at the Toronto airport. Toronto — or Graysville, as I had come to call it — had left an unpleasant smoggy taste in my mouth, a taste I was looking forward to drowning with a couple of ice-cold Palliser Pale Ales as soon as I got home. To say I had not enjoyed myself would be an understatement. Four whole days in Jack's company had turned out to be a struggle to say the least, and I was more than ready to return to western civilization, a view of the mountains, that big sky. How Ontarians — that is what they call themselves, isn't it? — can survive their landscape is beyond me. It made me feel claustrophobic, everything so small, the trees crowding in. Jack said he thought that mountains were a lot more menacing, the way they loom over you, all that cold hard rock. He went so far as to call them sinister. Sinister? It's Ontario that's sinister.

To tell you the truth, I had no overwhelming desire to

visit Toronto in the first place, but I was curious about Jack. He and I had been e-mailing almost daily for the past year, had struck up quite the little long-distance romance, and agreed that it was time for us to meet. When he suggested an all-expenses-paid trip east, I couldn't refuse. It was generous of him, really. The possibility of sex was a given if we clicked, so that was one less thing to worry about. But it came as a shock that as attractive as Jack was physically, my ex-husband's company had been easier to take. Darryl and I began our twenty-year marriage with a bang — I've always found older men irresistible — but, as my friend Rita joked, it ended with a wimp: Darryl, an old man cocooned in his armchair, lost in a book. But I'll say one thing for Darryl: at least he knew how to shut up sometimes. Jack just talks and talks.

Everyone I knew, my parents included, called Darryl "a good catch" as if he were some sort of prize trout, which I guess he was. There was definitely something fishy about him, for instance the niggling little detail that he had reached forty without ever having married. Without even having lived with anyone, in fact. His prolonged bachelorhood had decided advantages, though; namely, the healthy savings account he brought with him. We were able to buy a house immediately — for cash — and I made sure he bought a good one, in the best part of town, a sound investment. It would help his career, I assured him, if he had a suitable address to which he could invite colleagues for dinner parties. Unlike me, who lived on tinned soups and crackers when I was on my own,

Darryl could actually cook and didn't mind doing so. Eventually, we would have kids (we ended up with three), so we might as well buy big at the outset and not have to move later.

It all went remarkably well at first. Darryl made plenty of money, so I quit my job clerking for the Ministry of Transportation where we had met. He'd come in to renew his driver's licence, and ended up with a wife. I'm back there working again since we split up. Not much has changed there except everything is computerized now.

Darryl was used to having plenty of time to himself, which suited me just fine. I needed space too. Having anyone, even someone I liked, in the same room with me for too long felt, well, too *close*. Made me want to get into my truck and drive, which I often did, west to Banff for a coffee or south to Nanton where I had relatives, or north to Red Deer or even as far up as Edmonton just for the hell of it. I didn't go east much; east has never been my favourite direction. Which should have been a warning about Jack, who was an easterner after all. But I didn't know this when we first met in an Internet chat room for Alberta buffs. Or buff Albertans as I was hoping, having been apart from Darryl for a few months by then.

Jack and I hit it off that very first afternoon. It was a rainy Sunday. I had come down with a cold and felt a pang of regret that Darryl wasn't there to make tea for me. Rita, a big fan of chat rooms as a dating service, phoned and said I should get right on the computer, there was an interesting-sounding guy going by the name Glacial

Erratic in the one she was in at that very moment. That caught my attention since I've always been intrigued by rocks, even as a child, and had been frequently to the Okotoks Erratic, which is only ten kilometres from Calgary. It's the largest glacial erratic in the world, weighing in at 16,500 tons. I'm still amazed that a melting glacier could carry such an enormous hunk of rock so many thousands of kilometres.

Anyway, it was easy to get talking to Glacial Erratic, who it seemed was well-informed about rocks. He knew about the Frank Slide of 1903, the most devastating avalanche in North American history. He knew that the lichen that grows on the boulders at the site is orange. He knew that quartz was once thought to be solidified light. He knew about the formation of the Waterton Lakes. He knew so much about southern Alberta that I had no idea for a while that he was, in fact, born and raised in Toronto. And it was only a while later, after several weeks on-line, that I learned his real name. To my surprise, it was one I recognized. He was a well-known journalist, but I didn't let on that I had heard of him, that I had even seen reviews in *The Calgary Herald* of his book on Native art. It wouldn't do to give him a swelled head. I didn't even tell him that I had read his *Maclean's* piece on the childhood summers he spent in the Crow's Nest Pass. No wonder he knew so much about rocks; his father had been a geologist.

Jack certainly doesn't need to worry about money or his career. He's told me that not only do all his pieces sell but magazines actually call *him* to assign him work. He doesn't even have to look for it.

Work is important for Jack. He views work as an end in itself, calls it "fulfilling." The very day I arrived in Toronto, he came up with a new writing assignment. "Joanne," he said, "I'd like to write a piece about how we met. Our on-line relationship and how it has developed over the past year. A personal piece, something that focuses on just the two of us. What do you think? Lots of people would be interested since Internet romances seem to be the way to go these days."

I was flattered, sure, and I figured it wouldn't be too hard to sit back and let him do it — after all, I wouldn't have to lift a finger — so I agreed. Besides, it was amusing to imagine Darryl reading it. And I'd make sure he knew about it. Of course, Jack, as the writer, would probably get all the glory, but maybe some of it would rub off. After all, it had happened to Mona Lisa, hadn't it? Leonardo painted her, and now she's the most recognized woman in the history of art.

After our first dinner, we had what I think of as introductory sex, the exciting but slightly awkward first-time sex with a new partner. I've been through this a number of times now, especially since I left Darryl, and it's always the same, the peering over the coffee cup the next morning wondering if he enjoyed it as much as I had, or less, or more, or not at all. Once the initial sex was out of the way, things got a bit more relaxed, at least in that department. Jack was an early riser, so he served me breakfast in bed. He did like to talk though, kept insisting that we should get to know each other now that we were together in "real time," as he put it. I would have preferred less talk and more sex, especially since his conversation was not exactly scintillating. He went on endlessly about focus and goals and discipline. I told him that my philosophy was to get through life by exerting as little energy as possible. "Like rocks," I said. He looked as though he was about to say something but changed his mind. My remark did make him stop talking though, at least for a minute.

By Day Two, I had heard enough about his work and his trips and his ex-wife and his estranged kids to last me a lifetime. His cat was getting on my nerves too, kept jumping on my lap every time I sat down. But it was the stats that did me in. He'd researched Internet dating services, who used them and how often and to what end. The more numbers he listed, the more I needed air, desperately. I knew the only way I was going to get it was to insist on doing some sightseeing on my own. "You can work on your piece, and I'll just go look around for a few hours. Keep out of your way. I'll be back for dinner though." He had made a delicious pork roast the night before, and I was hoping his culinary performance would be repeated. I've always been a sucker for men who cook. I remember how Darryl used to sit me in a chair with a beer while he pitched the tent and then made a wonderful dinner on the campfire. It was fascinating to watch how much he could do in an hour.

I also have a secret addiction to Big Macs. I get a real hankering sometimes, even go out at two a.m. occasionally to get one. I hadn't indulged for several days now, so it was time to find a McDonald's, and Jack, who had just yesterday railed about the empty calories in fast food, did not need to know about it.

It was while I was enjoying a Big Mac with an extra-large order of fries and an extra-large Coke that I had a superb idea. I find my brain usually works best while I'm eating. While I was here I would help Jack write his article. I don't know why I hadn't thought of this right away. I had always fantasized about being a writer. Writers have such glamorous lives, and writing can't be all that hard really. I've put words to paper before, written hundreds of messages on e-mail. If I helped Jack write the piece, I'd be more directly a part of it, and we'd share the byline. It would be more equal if we collaborated, Mona and Leonardo, not just Leonardo. We could start tonight, and we still had two days. Besides, Jack could do all the revising and editing after I was gone, and e-mail the final draft for my approval.

The more I thought about it, the more excited I got. Fame would be fun. I imagined the interviews — my voice on the radio, my face on TV, my graceful ascension to the stage at the National Magazine Awards to accept first prize. *The Calgary Herald* would come calling, as would *The Globe and Mail* and *The National Post* and *Maclean's*. I could start writing pieces on my own, and Jack could help me get them published. There had been a reason the Internet brought us together. It was fate.

I hurried back to Jack's place. "I thought you weren't going to be back till dinner," he said, not entirely pleased by my early reappearance.

"I've had a great idea. I'm going to work with you." I could barely contain my excitement.

"Work with me?" He obviously had no clue.

"Yes, work with you," I said, my grin a mile wide. "On your article. The one about us."

"Oh."

"We can start right away. Come on. I'll join you at the computer."

"But I've already started. I've been working on it ever since you left."

"Well, we'll just start again."

"But, Joanne, what do you know about writing?"

I didn't appreciate his condescending tone and began to feel annoyed. "A lot more than you think. I read all sorts of magazines and newspapers. I read every day. I write lots on the computer."

"But as I said, I've already started the piece. In fact, I've finished it."

"Finished it?"

"Uh-huh."

"You must've done a pretty rushed job then. Are you going to show it to me?"

"Sure."

He ambled over to the computer. As I sat there on his battered plaid couch and listened to the paper slide out of the printer, I decided I didn't like him very much. He handed me the pages and then went off to the kitchen to get us drinks. I read the piece, and thought it was good, though hell would freeze over before I'd ever tell him that. It was quite acceptably complimentary to me, actually, which I didn't mind. I wouldn't tell him that either.

"So what do you think?" he asked, after I had finished.

"It's okay," I said.

"I'll still need to do revisions. But is it all right if I publish it?"

"I don't know. I'll have to think about it."

"I can change your name if you want, make the whole thing less personal."

"No, you can leave all that alone." I'd be damned if he told my story and didn't attach my name to it, one way or another.

"Fine, then. I'll e-mail you the final version when you get back to Calgary." Which couldn't be soon enough as far as I was concerned.

Our last day together was strained, and I kept wishing I had booked an earlier flight. It didn't leave until four so I thought we could at least have a last roll in the hay, but for some reason Jack wasn't interested. His loss. We ended up reading newspapers all morning and he, of course, had a comment to make about every piece he read. And then, to top it off, we got into an argument on the way to the airport because of his reckless driving. The way he wove in and out of traffic it's a wonder we got there in one piece. It was like he was trying to win a race or something, he was in such a rush.

I felt an immense relief when the plane lifted, heading west. I decided that I would stay in touch with Jack for a while longer, eventually give him permission to publish the article, but not without making him sweat a bit first. And when it appeared, the entire country would know my name, coupled with his. Like Mona and Leonardo, forever and ever.

Extreme Makeover

What strikes me right away as I sit down at our usual table is the flamingo arrangement at the centre of the room. The absurd flock, about a dozen in all, weren't here last week, but they're sure here now. You can't miss them. Plastic impostors twisted into all sorts of unnatural shapes, an impossible synthetic pink. I can't imagine why Chris has added them to the décor, as if the place weren't weird enough already. He's got some urban nautical theme going: life jackets, shells, ships' flags, nets, things like that. There's even a plush purple octopus suspended in a corner. I wonder where he found one so large. How the flamingos are supposed to fit in with this, I have no idea. And real flamingos are not garish like this lot. They're a vivid coral red, at least the ones I've seen, and quite compelling. Ugly and beautiful at the same time with those graceful question mark necks.

Tacky as the place is, Josie and I have been getting to-gether for drinks at the Anchor Bar and Grill (you guessed it, there's an anchor on the wall) every Thursday night for the past few months — ever since I got a job at the Salamander Gallery, just down the street from her office. It's the closest bar to meet at after work, and the chairs are comfortable, with cushioned seats and armrests. We decided it would be a fun way to get an early start on the weekend. Josie is as punctual as I am, and today's no different. It's five on the dot, and here she is, looking, as always, as if she's just stepped out of some fashion magazine. Guys, to use one of our old high school expressions, drool over her. She's actually gotten more attractive with age, not that thirty is old, but you know what I mean. And having money doesn't hurt. She makes a bundle working for her dad's market research company. I figure she'll take over completely when he retires.

We exchange the usual hi-how-are-yous and she sits down, sweeps the hair from her face. She looks uncharacteristically flushed. Flustered almost. The waiter — new, like the flamingo disaster — saunters over, and I ask him if Chris is around (I'm itching to complain about the ongoing aesthetic decline of the place), but he's not. So I settle for ordering drinks, a glass of merlot for Josie and a gingerale for me. I'd ordinarily have a beer, but I've been trying to cut down on the calories ever since the zipper on my jeans refused to do up. At first I blamed it on the dryer, but when all the other zippers misbehaved, I had to face it: the clothes hadn't shrunk. I had expanded.

"What's with the gingerale?" she asks.

"Not as many calories as beer."

"Don't kid yourself. Gingerale has sugar in it. It's got almost as many calories as beer."

I've learned over the years not to argue with Josie when it comes to this sort of information. She's a walking encyclopedia of product statistics.

Although Josie and I talk about all sorts of things, one of our favourite subjects is the importance of not letting ourselves go. We're worried that we'll end up like our mothers, overweight and looking older than we are. There's nothing wrong with being the best you can be, that's our philosophy. So, when she announces she's got big news and it involves self-improvement, I'm already in favour of it. I'm assuming she's going to enrol in a yoga class or join a book club. Change her hair colour. Or maybe break up with Ted, her live-in boyfriend of the past two years. I wouldn't be surprised. She's been complaining a lot about him lately. Mostly about how he doesn't pay enough attention to her. They hardly ever have sex, and she keeps catching him ogling other women. Her word, ogling. It makes me think of dangling eyeballs, but I resist saying this. After all, we're planning to have dinner later. No use killing the appetite. Then again, it might help with the zipper situation.

As the drinks arrive, Josie finally tunes in to the flamingos. "Oh my god! What is Chris *thinking*? Look at those things! They look like they came from Dollar Mart."

I grin. This is one of the things I've always liked about Josie. She makes me laugh. She's *always* made me laugh.

Lisa and Josie — or Lise and Jose as we've called each other since we met in Grade Nine — we're an odd pair really. If you were sitting at the next table, you'd see two women, one with chin-length dark hair in a designer business suit, skirt just the right length; the other, with spiky blonde hair in a red tank top and blue jeans sporting a small Bart Simpson tattoo on her right shoulder. The jeans girl is me. I may look the part, but it's really Josie who's the wild one. She's always masked it well, though. Even my parents thought she was wonderful. "Such a polite girl," my mother wistfully remarked on more than one occasion, as if her daughter wasn't. The fact that Josie had straight *A*'s was useful too. It meant my parents didn't hassle me about all the time we spent hanging out together, and they didn't ask too many questions. Parents like it when their kids have smart friends.

We had some good times, *great* times really. Like the weekend in Grade Twelve when we went to Montreal together to visit my brother Dave at McGill. His buddies almost fell over each other trying to sit next to Josie when we went out. Even Dave wasn't immune. I'm convinced that the only reason he didn't try to hit on her was that she was my best friend. He was afraid she'd tell me everything, including details no sister should know.

I knew plenty about Josie that no one else knew. I knew, for instance, that she went on the Pill in Grade Ten because her first-ever boyfriend Matt had convinced her that he just couldn't live without sex and would find it elsewhere if not with her. I also knew that she and Matt were having oral sex — and learned that, unlike our oral presentations in English, it had nothing to do with talking. Jose was quite a source of information, and I listened intently, realizing that I had much to learn. But even back then I was good at putting on the tough act to cover up the truth: I was shy.

"You've got to please a man, Lise, and then you can get him to do what you want." She sounded — though I didn't realize this at the time — like an advice columnist from a back-issue of *Cosmo*, or worse, like my mother's oldest sister. Aunt Marian believed firmly in the concept of behind-the-throne rule. Power was a matter of perception: you could have more of it when it appeared that you had none. But, as I said, I didn't know any of this in those days. Josie had what I wanted and couldn't seem to get for myself: experience.

"You think the flamingos are odd?" I take a large swig of gingerale before I continue. "Did you read the paper yesterday? Somebody actually paid nearly two thousand U.S. for a perogi that looks like an image of Jesus! It showed up in Toledo in some woman's frying pan. Can you believe it? The face of Christ scorched into a dumpling? There was even a picture of it. The reporter thought it looked like Charles Manson. I thought it looked like a burnt perogi. I guess I must be lacking in imagination. And then, right next to this, was an article about scientists turning pee into electricity."

"Get serious."

"I'm not kidding! They've invented urine-powered batteries. Heh, maybe the next thing will be urine-powered cars! We can pee into our gas tanks. It sure would be cheaper!"

By this point, Josie is laughing. "Jesus, Lise!"

"You must have me confused with a perogi!"

More laughter. We can hardly stop. When we calm down a notch, I bring the conversation back to the Big News. She's got me curious.

"So what's up, Jose? Are you breaking up with Ted?"

"Nope. Quite the contrary. I think our relationship is about to improve."

"How so? You guys going for counselling?" (Fat chance, but I thought I'd ask anyway.)

"No. I'm going to give myself a little gift and in the process give him one, too."

"What are you talking about?"

"Are you ready for this?"

"Is the gingerale strong enough? Will I need a beer?"

"You might."

By now she has me totally intrigued. Josie has always been good at this sort of thing. Attention build-up. She has drama queen possibilities.

"I'm getting a makeover."

"Oh," I say, having expected something more earth-shattering. "New make-up? Getting your hair cut?"

"No. It's a different sort of makeover."

"You're getting a new personality?" I can never resist a smart-ass remark.

"I'm getting…." She pauses. Looks away in the direction of the flamingos. "I'm getting a genital makeover."

"A *what?*" I might as well be reading about perogis and urine-powered batteries. This is right up there. And where is the waiter? I wave furiously in his direction. This definitely calls for a beer.

"I've been thinking about it for a while now, ever since Ted showed me an article he saw in the paper. He's all for it. Says it'll improve our sex life."

"What does a genital makeover" — I can hardly say the words — "involve exactly?"

"Dr. Latky — he's the specialist I've been seeing — says it'll take a couple of days in the hospital and then about six weeks of recovery time."

"No, Jose. I mean what exactly will it *involve?*"

"He'll tighten things up, do a little tucking. Make things more symmetrical. You know."

Before I can tell her that I sure as hell *don't* know, the waiter materializes.

"Are you getting a facelift?" he says, with a friendly lilt in his voice. "Pardon me for overhearing, but my boyfriend is thinking about getting one too. I'm trying to talk him out of it though."

"Oh," I say. "Hmmm." Too much information.

"Could you bring her a Coors Light please? And me another merlot? Thanks." Josie, efficient as always. After the waiter is out of earshot, I try again.

"Okay, Jose. Let's see if I'm getting this. You've been seeing some guy who specializes in genital makeovers.

And you're going to have one."

"Uh-huh. He's an artist, Lise. I read some of the testimonials. One woman called him the Picasso of vaginas." Josie wasn't usually prone to this sort of gushing. It was unnerving. And I couldn't help but think of Judy Chicago's *Dinner Party* plates and Georgia O'Keefe's flowers. I've always found this overt genitalia stuff a bit much.

"What does he practice on? Not canvas, I presume."

Josie's response to my question took me off guard. "No, actually, I read on the Internet that he practises on animal parts. Chicken thighs, turkey legs, pig's ears. Whatever works I guess."

"*Pig's ears?*"

"Yeah, it was all in the article."

The waiter returns, puts the drinks in front of us. He smiles before departing. I ignore the glass and take a healthy swig from the bottle. The beer is ice cold, and more satisfying than the gingerale.

"Don't worry, Lise. He's got an excellent reputation. He's done dozens of these makeovers. He's even franchising the operation."

I decide at that moment that some of the most ridiculous conversations in the world take place across restaurant tables.

"Jose," I say, "aren't you worried about the risk? Infections? What if he makes a mistake? And what about the pain?"

"Dr. Latky says it'll be worth it. He says he's had husbands and boyfriends send him thank-you gifts."

"Yeah, I bet."

"It's also about aesthetics. And self-esteem. Dr. Latky says that if you know you look good down there, it makes you more comfortable. Then you enjoy sex more. He says he can create perfection, just like what you see in *Playboy*."

"You're kidding, right? Jose, when have *you* ever had problems with self-esteem?" She's sounding brainwashed. Or brain-dead. I'm not sure which.

"I'm not getting any younger, Lise." Josie is almost apologetic. "I just want to feel good, and I want Ted to be excited when he's with me. When I know he's turned on, it turns *me* on. Dr. Latky says that some women are so loose you could fit an alarm clock into them. I don't want to be one of them."

"That's gross!" I'm starting to get worked up.

"But true."

"Yeah, well whole babies can fit in there too. Maybe that's the point. Maybe a little space is needed."

"You know I'm not having any kids. I decided that back in high school. So that's not an issue for me. After I recover from the operation, Ted and I are going away for a lovers' holiday. It should be fantastic!"

"Has he ever considered enlarging himself rather than shrinking you?"

"You don't understand, Lise. This is for me. I *want* to do it." She looks away from me to the flamingos.

I continue to watch her for a long moment. I have known Josie for half of my life. I remember the hours we spent in Grade Nine asking question after question of her Ouija board as we gulped Cokes in the newly renovated basement of her house. *How old will I be when I get married? What will be the initials of the man I marry? What colour hair will he have? Will I have any kids? How many? What city will I live in?* I recall the touching earnestness with which we interrogated the universe about our futures. We could not have imagined the topics that concern us now. The faces of deities on food stuffs. Urine power. Designer vaginas. I want to be flippant, but for some reason I can't be.

Josie turns her attention back to the flamingos and smiles. "You know, Lise, they're not half bad when you get used to them."

The Art of Dying

For those who seek to understand it, death is a highly creative force.   —Elisabeth Kübler-Ross

"So are you nervous?" you ask, as you change radio stations. I admire your firm hand on the wheel, how your heavy gold ring catches the January sunlight. It is the twin, of the one I myself am wearing.

"Nervous about what?"

"Seeing corpses. Are you sure you're going to be okay with this exhibit? I know how squeamish you are."

"I'll be fine," I say, and for some reason, I actually believe it. The squeamish part is certainly true though. I've been known to faint at the sight of my own blood in a lab syringe — and I don't like the word "corpses." It makes me think of gross decomposition, people pulled apart, horrific and frightening. Despite this, going to the Body Worlds show in Toronto was my idea.

The show received a lot of publicity, and I thought I should face the facts, so to speak; namely my own mortality, which is a subject I'm generally not fond of considering.

"They're not really corpses anyway," you say. "The Science Centre write-up calls them 'plastinated' figures. In the photographs, they don't even look real. They look like they've been made for a horror movie by a special-effects team."

It occurs to me that in the almost five years we've lived together, we've rarely discussed death. Maybe because we've been so busy living. Or maybe because it's not my favourite topic. Or maybe we haven't talked about it simply because it doesn't seem to concern you much.

"So what do you think happens after we die?" I say.

"Nothing. When we're dead, we're dead."

I shift my gaze from the truck barrelling along perilously close to us to your profile. *Patrician*, an artist acquaintance who had known you in your thirties called it recently. He couldn't believe you had turned fifty since he had last seen you. I myself can't quite believe it. I'm younger than you by ten years, but I think of you as so full of life, so adventurous, that I tend to forget the age difference.

"Gwen, are you afraid of death?"

"Not at all," you say. "And I'm not into prolonging it either. If I had a terminal illness, I'd go to the Arctic and walk into oblivion."

I smile. "You'd better not be doing that just yet. We've got our dream home to move into in a few months."

Without taking your eyes off the road, you reach for the radio again and this time turn it off. "I don't know why you're so excited about it, Sara. It's just a house."

I'm not used to such coolness from you, and my stomach tightens with an unexpected anxiety, which I try to ignore. You're probably just tired. You did say this morning that you hadn't been sleeping well lately.

Early in our relationship, you wrote: *What we have together is amazing to me. I'm trying to believe it all without fleeing from it.* I repeat the words to myself, now, years later: *without fleeing.* How could I not have noticed these words when you wrote them?

It is the end of May and unseasonably warm when we move into our just-completed new house. We had been planning to buy a place together ever since you moved into mine, and now we're finally here, in our own home, chosen together. Home. The word is a nest, soft and comforting. It conjures images of down duvets and over-sized pillows and languid hours of love-making.

The furniture won't arrive until next week, but we have plenty of boxes to unpack. These have kept us busy all morning, and we're both pleased by how many of the small items we've already found places for: the cat brush, the fondue fuel, my camera, your deck of cards for Solitaire. We've hung the shower curtains in both bathrooms, created a temporary bed out of camping foam, and organized the kitchen, which is bright and spacious. We talk of how much we'll enjoy cooking in it together.

You place the single yellow rose in its blue glass vase — a moving-in gift from the builder — on the mantel. I put bottles in the wine rack. Light floods through the floor-to-ceiling living room window. The window is mirrored in the smooth polished oak floor. A song you've always liked comes on the radio: *To really love a woman, to understand her, you gotta know her deep inside. Hear every thought, see every dream, and give her wings when she wants to fly.* You pull me to you, lead me to the centre of the room, and we begin to dance slowly, easily. Since we're the same height, our bodies fit together like two halves of the same whole, connected and sensual. When I kiss your neck, I taste salt. I've heard that salt water doesn't freeze. I don't know why I think of this. *When you love a woman you tell her that she's the one. Cuz she needs somebody to tell her that it's gonna last forever.* You, not the building, are my home.

Five days later. Days. Five. I still reel when I think of it. Five days later, you announce that you're leaving. You say that you can't live with me, that I'm too emotional, too social, too talkative, too energetic. Too everything. You say I overwhelm you. You say you want the furniture delivery cancelled and the house sold. You kill our relationship with an awesome detachment. (A friend will later say that you remind her of an iceberg: cold, hard, and formidable. Dangerously hidden, only the tip visible.) When I call you *brutal* and *merciless,* the words slide off you without penetrating.

Your leaving seems sudden only because I've been oblivious to the fact that it's been going on for months. It's been a process, a gradual withdrawal, pushed along by increasingly frequent arguments. *Moving on*, you called it when you told me about how you'd left others, but I bclieved you when you said I was your last stop, the one you'd travelled toward for a lifetime. I did not know that you were such an accomplished performer.

You practised your departure over and over, going farther each time. You let yourself go gradually. *Soft release*, bird experts call it. A bird is released, brought back in, released again. The time that it flies free is progressively increased. Each rehearsal is longer than the last. When the final flight happens, it's a surprise even though it has been expected. The bird takes off and doesn't look back. This is how you released yourself from me.

What happens next is beyond comprehension. You do your best to cut me not only from your life, but from your mind. You don't allow your friends to mention my name. You cease all communication with me except for perfunctory e-mail about business matters. As soon as the house is sold, even that will end. I'll never know why you didn't give us a chance in the new house, and when you made your decision. I'll never know at what moment love became non-love, and commitment became escape.

I need to understand, and you need me not to. Your needs are about making way for your next drama. In order to survive, you need to erase me. Once you have re-created yourself, you will seduce a new audience, one that is unfamiliar with your past performances. An audience who will not question the script you've chosen or notice that, yet again, you're playing the victim lead.

You will resurrect me later, but only after the new play has opened, and not in my original role. You will cast me as a lover turned villain, complete with all the requisite transgressions. You will twist the truth, gain sympathy, entertain strangers with fictions about my behaviour. Meanwhile, your own behaviour will remain unacknowledged and conveniently buried.

I'm not the first person you've re-cast in this way, and I doubt I'll be the last.

On our first anniversary you wrote: *Regardless of what happens, even if we should one day part, this ring will stay on my finger forever. It is my commitment to you, the wonderful person you are.* Many things can be committed. People. Crimes. And you've always been fond of the concept of "forever." You promise it to all your partners, each one in succession. I wonder where the ring is now, to what fate it has been committed.

* * *

You've asked me to stop talking so you can focus on the traffic, which has grown increasingly heavy since we passed Oakville. You've requested silence a lot lately, and what you vaguely call "space." Simple tasks such as buying groceries have come to tax you. If the phone rings twice in a row, you get upset. Your fragility is like a hairline crack in the ice, barely visible at first, but growing. There are only two ways for you to solve this: freeze solid or melt entirely. As the weeks pass, you will opt for freezing. When your brother dies in May, you don't cry.

The Body Worlds exhibit surprises me but doesn't. It's a paradox, a matter of holding two opposing ideas at the same time, in this case the notion that one moment a person is alive, and the next, dead. Instant transformation.

The corridor leading to the whole-body display area is lined with glass cases filled with small exhibits, tame ones, of hip and knee replacements, elbow joints, bones mostly. I think of it as the warm-up act. It's like stepping into a hot bath gradually, one foot first, getting acclimatized.

Once we get beyond the entrance, the place feels more like an art gallery than a science centre. There is no formaldehyde smell, no blood, nothing wet or messy. The bodies, injected with plastic — bright Play Dough colours, atlas blue and bubblegum pink — seem safely artificial. I have to keep reminding myself that these specimens were once breathing people with names and thoughts. They have now been reduced to the sum of their separate physical parts, unique yet universal in their anonymous humanity.

Each figure is a sculpture. "The Angel" poses with her shoulder muscles flayed and spread to look like wings. "The Thinker" reminds me of Rodin. "The Exploded Man" is a mobile, all his individual parts suspended around him on nylon threads.

Some of the bodies have been cross-sectioned into slices. I picture them hanging from a window, like stained glass. I imagine the sun shining through their organs, throwing patterns on the wall.

We stand for what seems like a long time in front of "The Drawer Man." Doors have been cut into his body, and his chest hangs open like a cupboard. I stare at his halved heart so intently that I don't notice you move on to the next figure.

Moving in, moving out, moving on. It's the preposition that makes the difference.

* * *

Your words from the end of our fourth year together: *I'm writing this to tell you how beneficial it has been for me to live with someone as cheerful as you. As you know, I can get down sometimes, but your positive outlook helps keep me afloat.* But, you should have added, eventually none of this will be enough. You should have warned me that cheerful would become *too* cheerful. You should have warned me that your return to Prozac would not solve your problem, that the scales would tip, and no amount of love would prevent them from doing so.

* * *

It's now July, and you're gone. Before you took up temporary residence at a friend's place, you piled your belongings into what would have been your office at our new house. Soon you will take them to your new apartment. What you deliberately left behind: my favourite bird feeder, the photo album that contained only pictures of us, the plant-box I gave you just days before we became lovers.

I have spent the last few days living my life in reverse, moving back to my original home, the one you've shared with me since we began. I'm grateful that I delayed putting it on the market and that it's still there, a remnant of safety. I've emptied cupboards and closets. I've re-packed the dishes, cutlery and placemats. I've boxed my books, bagged my clothes, and removed the bottles from the wine rack. I've hauled carloads of items back to the house I was looking forward to leaving.

This is my last trip. I don't touch the rose on the mantel, though it has dried and shrivelled. I remember to check all the drawers. When I come across your Solitaire deck in one of them, I take it down to your office where, on impulse, I remove two cards. When tomorrow you arrive to collect your things, you'll see them on your ironing board: the Queen of Spades topping the Queen of Hearts. I guess I've known it all along really: one way or another, death trumps love, every time. But you're wrong about what happens afterward. There's life after all, just of a different kind.

Truth

Today is my fiftieth birthday. As I stand here before the merciless bathroom mirror, I can no longer avoid the truth: my roots are showing and what they're showing is how gray my hair has become. I've been fighting the gray army for years — started highlighting in my mid-twenties — but, I must confess, I'm tired of the battle, which I'm losing anyway. So, as of this moment, I'm no longer colouring my hair. No more lengthy, expensive hair treatments. No more finding space on the calendar for increasingly frequent appointments. I'm going to show my true colours, untinted.

Jenn and Leslie are coming for lunch at noon. I know what they will think of the hair idea — "hare-brained" Jenn will say and Leslie will agree — but I'm telling them anyway. They've already been introduced to some of my other recent changes; for example, my frequent use of terms such as *downsize*, *simplicity*, and *uncluttered*. They've watched with undisguised bewilderment my gradual unloading of household items, which started with my sudden (although not totally unexpected) unloading of Larry, my husband of twenty-five years, to our young dental hygienist, blue-eyed and white-smocked, who had become far more interested in his mouth than I was. My life instantly became half as big and twice as manageable. And certainly simpler and less cluttered.

Once he was gone, I began to divest myself of furniture and all the domestic non-essentials I had whim by whim accumulated. I gave away a dining room table and six chairs, a recently re-upholstered couch, two bookcases along with the paperbacks, a dozen empty picture frames, kitchen gadgets, pillows. Everything left quietly and without protest. I was amazed at how easy it was to give things away. My sister's university-bound children were fair game for my generosity — my niece started calling me the Blessed Lady of Largesse — as was the local women's shelter. I didn't have the patience for garage sales.

Jenn and Leslie watched the gradual diminishment of my material possessions with interest but without comprehension. The time would come, I assured them, when they too would embrace what I had taken to calling the Reversal of Acquisition. What they didn't know was that, unfortunately, my newfound urge to unburden myself applied only to the material world, and that a strange new compulsion had taken its place. Instead of settling for checking my e-mail each morning as I had done prior to Larry's departure, I had become addicted to Google.

When it came to amassing facts, I had never felt more acquisitive. I realized that my nature really did abhor a vacuum. One minute I was bagging clothes for the Salvation Army; the next I was passionately gathering details, tossing them together in my brain as if it were a Cuisinart. Fascinating, how the mind operates, making its own unexpected connections. As I began paying attention to the order of my seemingly random entries into the Google search engine, I became aware that my unconscious was making choices. I found patterns emerging, and I could map the routes my mind would take. Recently, for instance, I went from the history of Revlon to eighteenth-century wigs to Mozart's childhood to Viennese architecture to Freud to Cuban cigars to the sex life of sea horses and finally stopped at AIDS. One morning I even Googled Google.

Each day brought new information and the more I had, the more I wanted. I was insatiable. There seemed to be no logic to the subject choices, generated by my curious mind like icon line-ups in a slot machine viewing window. I'd enter a word or phrase, an almost instantaneous list of Web destinations would appear, and then I'd be off, jumping from site to site in gleeful abandon like a caffeinated cyber frog. It was the ultimate in collecting, this gathering of detail, which I didn't consider at all trivial. Every bit of it mattered somewhere, to someone. And best of all it didn't take up space, at least not in my house.

My day doesn't seem complete now without my morning computer ritual. Along with the requisite seven a.m. coffee comes the inevitable Googling. I can't leave for the office until I've had my fix. It's immensely seductive, the sense that knowledge with a capital K is out there and it can be mine if I just type in a word or two.

Yesterday I received a postcard from a vacationing colleague in the federal taxation department, where I work. It's a picture of a white alligator. I had no idea such a thing even existed, so I begin this morning's Internet journey by typing in "white alligator."

White alligators are not albino. They lack pigment in their skin but have colour in their eyes. An albino's eyes are pink, showing the tiny blood vessels below the surface, but white alligators have brilliant blue eyes. Their hide looks like white chocolate. In 1987, Louisiana environmentalists were amazed to find eighteen white alligators all hatched in one nest. It is the only white alligator find in recorded history. Since all of the hatchlings were male, they have no mates of their own coloration. In captivity, alligators can live up to eighty years.

The white chocolate reference makes me think of dessert. My favourite is lemon cake which I'm likely to have later, at the party Leslie and Jenn are throwing for me this evening. But I don't know much about lemons except that they grow on trees. "Lemon trees," I type, and learn that they, too, can live up to eighty years. There's more, of course. There's always more.

On the Amalfi Coast, home of limoncello liqueur, Sfusato Amalfitano lemons — distinguished by their pointed shape, pale yellow rind and intense aroma — are grown on tiny strips of tiered land overlooking the Tyrrhenian Sea. Narrow roads wind their way around rugged precipices. Clear azure water laps against craggy black rocks. Magenta bougainvillea and lush green ivy cascade down steep walls. Carved into the hillsides: faded pastel houses and terraces of lemon groves, whose fragrance is pervasive.

I consider Googling white chocolate, Louisiana, limoncello, and the Tyrrhenian Sea. All this Italy stuff reminds me of Larry's friend Mario, the best man at our wedding. Mario Ponzo, whose name, Larry explained to me the day I was first introduced to Mario, was amusing because there was another Mario Ponzo, the one after whom the Ponzo Illusion is named. I can't remember exactly what the Ponzo Illusion is, but there's an easy way to find out.

In 1913 Mario Ponzo drew his famous perception illustration: two identical lines converging like railroad tracks, and across them, two bars. The upper bar appears much larger because it spans a greater apparent distance between the rails. In fact, the two bars are the same width. The theory is that the background of what we see affects how we see it.

Sounds like something smart people know, and whenever I think of smart, I can't help but think of Susan Sontag. Now *there* was a brain crammed full to brimming! And so I'm off again. Because Susan Sontag died fairly recently, just before Christmas, I look up her obituaries, careful to put her name in quotation marks so that I won't get entries for a thousand Susans who are not Sontag and the few Sontags who are not Susan. (I've always thought of her as a hyphenated being anyway, Susan-Sontag, never the first name without the last or vice versa.) There are, of course, all the usual lists of accomplishments, publications, and biographical data, the flotsam and jetsam of a celebrated life, but as I read I become more interested in the personal details and in her own remarks, some of which surface as quotes in the vast sea of reminiscences.

In 1969, she was spotted buying several pints of Häagen-Dazs in a New York bodega near the corner of 103rd Street and Broadway. Although I resist checking out Broadway and bodegas and the history of New York, I do take a detour to Häagen-Dazs, which I learn was founded by a young New York entrepreneur named Reuben Mattus who, in 1961, turned his mother's horse-and-buggy ice cream business into the one we know today.

Susan Sontag once confessed: *To be a polymath is to be interested in everything — and in nothing else.*

Her personal library, estimated to be between 20,000 and 25,000 volumes, ended up at UCLA. (UCLA: *University of California, Los Angeles. Founded in 1919. School colours: blue and gold. Comprises 174 buildings on 419* acres. *Undergrad programs: 118. Grad programs: 200. Faculty members: 3326.)*

Piranesi prints hung on her apartment walls. (Piranesi: *Renowned 18th Century Italian printmaker and architect best known for his series of etchings of Rome.)*

She liked to eat takeout mezze. (Mezze: *A Middle Eastern spread of numerous small tasty dishes.)*

She frequented the Russian Samovar. (Russian Samovar: *A restaurant and bar at 256 W. 52nd Street featuring a variety of flavoured vodkas and a piano player who looks like Lenin.* Vodka: *A strong, clear, typically colourless liquor, usually distilled from fermented grain, which leaves no smell of liquor on the breath.* Lenin: *Russian revolutionary, the founder of Bolshevism and the major force behind the Revolution of October 1917.)*

Reminiscing about childhood family barbecues, Susan Sontag said: *I ate and ate…. I was always hungry.*

The *New York Times* obit described her as *approachable, aloof, anticlimactic, original, derivative, naïve, sophisticated, condescending, populist, puritanical, sybaritic, sincere, posturing, ascetic, voluptuary, right-wing, left-wing, profound, superficial, ardent, bloodless, dogmatic, ambivalent, lucid, inscrutable, visceral, reasoned, chilly, effusive, relevant, passé, ambivalent, tenacious, ecstatic, melancholic, humorous, humourless, deadpan, rhapsodic, cantankerous and clever.* No one ever called her dull. As far as lists went, this was a pretty good one. But it left out "mortal" and "immortal."

Susan Sontag told a friend: *I want to experience my own*

death. She said she was glad she was dying consciously of cancer rather than dying unexpectedly in her sleep.

To a young man who asked her after one of her readings what she was most noted for, she said: *The white streak in my black hair.* The power of hair. Cat Stevens, in my youth, sang about the power growing in his hair. I loved that song, took it seriously much to my parents' chagrin. They were always after me to cut the unruly, frizzy cascade that hung well past my shoulders. I stubbornly refused, as I refuse now. My hair might be going gray, but I sure as hell have lots of it. This is a good thing. I figure when it comes to hair, it's the quantity, not colour, that counts.

Where to next? Susan Sontag elicits so many possible directions it's hard to decide. Chemotherapy? War photography? French cinema? Annie Leibovitz? Oscar Wilde?

I sit staring at the Susan Sontag quote still on the screen: *The truth is always something that is told, not something that is known. If there were no speaking or writing, there would be no truth about anything. There would only be what is.*

Suddenly, it's the moment I've been unknowingly Googling toward for months.

Truth.

I type in the magnificent, all-encompassing, mysterious word and hit *Enter.* In less than a second the first ten of 55,900,000 entries pop up on the screen. Of course, I don't stop at ten. Truth or Fiction. Operation

Truth. Truth Hardware. Soldiers for the Truth. Truth for
Life. The Awful Truth. Dial-the-Truth. The Truth about
George W. Bush. Kids 4 Truth. Welcome to Truth Aquat-
ics. Texans for Truth. The Truth about Hell. Truth, War
and Consequences. Prozac Truth. Pleasure Boat Captains
for Truth. Sword of Truth. Football Fans for Truth. The
Truth About Cheese. Petrified Truth. The Cosmic Church
of Truth. Guru Jeff's Page of Truth. Absolute Truth. The
Truth about Black Helicopters. The Fountain of Truth.
The Truth Shall Set You Free.

I finally stop scrolling after I pass the two hundred mark.
Jenn and Leslie will be arriving soon, and I haven't yet
made lunch. They won't mind though, will expect my
tardiness in fact. They know me well, as I know them. I
know they will want to sit outside in the garden despite
the heat. I also know they will both decline all alcoholic
beverages and ask for soda water with lemon. I'll be sure
not to put nuts in the salad because Jenn is allergic to
them. Leslie will be on time; Jenn will be fifteen minutes
early. We'll sit in our usual spots in the shade of the
large maple out back because Leslie, who's fair-skinned,
will want to avoid the sun. After complaining about the
weather, we'll have the requisite conversation about their
kids. I don't have any, so I'll politely feign interest in the
latest news about Leslie's two daughters, both still in
high school, and Jenn's son, a physics major at Queens.
When the offspring's activities have been given enough
conversation time, Leslie will begin ranting about some
article she's read in the morning paper. Jenn will try to

argue with her. After a few minutes, they will agree to disagree. I will smile. We're old friends growing older. Together.

I will put three boneless, skinless chicken breasts (no salt added) on the barbecue and ask them if they would like more soda. Leslie will make a comment about her increasing weight. Jenn will tell her in a mock British accent: "Girl, you look bloody great! When are you going to accept it?" At which point I'll calmly announce that I've accepted the truth of my aging and, as of today, I've stopped dyeing my hair. They'll groan and ask what on earth I'm thinking. *Don't you realize it will make you look old?* Perhaps I will tell them then about white alligators and lemon trees, about the life of Susan Sontag, about the significance of Ponzo and his illusion. The sky will remain cloudless and blue above us, hypnotically empty, making the world below seem suddenly clear, every blade of grass startling and true.

Eventually, we'll get around to eating. None of us will have seconds, not even of the salad. Leslie and Jenn will tactfully avoid talking about Larry and death and childless women and anything else they suspect might put a damper on my birthday mood. They will banter happily instead about which one of them will drive me to the party tonight, and I will bask in the warmth of their friendship.

I turn off the computer and head to the kitchen where I lay the cutting board on the counter and begin to slice the fruit for the soda. After a moment, knife suspended,

I pause and inhale deeply. *If there were no speaking or writing, there would be no truth about anything. There would only be what is.* Silence and the scent of lemons.

Acknowledgements

The words, by Barbara Bickel, in her collage *I Have Returned*:

I have entered the healing
power of the moon
growing it down around me
to enter the sacred womb
of the dark goddess and
turning pain into power
I have returned

It was writer Henry Miller who described Brassaï as having "no ordinary eyes." The source for the biographical information about Brassaï's relationship with his parents is *Letters to My Parents* by Brassaï, translated from the Hungarian by Peter Lai and Barna Kantor, The University of Chicago Press, 1997.

"Body and Soul" was published in *The Dalhousie Review* (Spring 2006), as was "Green Is the Most Difficult Colour (Spring 2007).

The lyrics quoted in "The Art of Dying" are from "Have You Ever Really Loved a Woman?" written by Adams/ Lange/Kaman, published by Badams Music Ltd./Zomba Entertprises Inc./K-man Corp./New Line Music Co., 1996, and sung by Bryan Adams.

I am grateful to the Ontario Arts Council for financial assistance during the writing of this book.

Thanks are long overdue to Jack Clark and Dorothy Farmiloe, two teachers whose encouragement during the earliest days of my writing life sowed a profound seed.

Thank you also to Marty Gervais for his support of my writing in general; to Elspeth Cameron for convincing me when I first began creating these stories that if I leapt, the net would appear (miraculously, it did); to Ricki Heller and Patricia Abram for their valuable insights on the first draft of the book and for their unwavering faith in it; to Joan Barfoot for reading the manuscript on very short notice and providing comments; to Anne Michaels for her kind remarks and her understanding of the heart-and-soulness of the writng process; to the "mentor extraordinaire" Isabel Huggan for her astute guidance during the revision stage; and to my son Brendan McCarney for always thinking of his mother as a "writer" (even during those times when it has been inconvenient for him to do so).

I would also like to thank my editor, Luciana Ricciutelli, for her enthusiastic birthing of this book into print.

Finally, a special thank-you to Constance Rennett for being Constance Rennett. Your love continues to alter me.

Eva Tihanyi's poetry:

About *Wresting the Grace of the World:*

"This exquisite little volume of poems is a joy from start to finish. Not that the subject matter is particularly joyful—but the poet's artistry engages the reader on every page.... Every once in a while you come across a book of poems that delights all the senses and satisfies the intellect at the same time. *Wresting the Grace of the World* is such a book. It deserves to be read and reread by those who appreciate poetry—and by those who don't."
—*Canadian Book Review Annual*

"You want from a book of poems what you want from a foreign country: strangeness and freshness. You want to restock depleted images, reprime the weary heart and rebrick damaged memory. You want the freshness of a new beginning, even if the roads travelled on—full of heartbreak and heartbloom—are as old as stone. Mellifluously voiced and naturally spoken, Eva Tihanyi's *Wresting the Grace of the World* delivers on all accounts."
—*Hammered Out*

Tihanyi's work is "sharply focused and often insightful, like a photo taken at a revealing moment."
—*Toronto Star*

About *Restoring the Wickedness:*

"This is a very accomplished, beautifully crafted collection of poems."
—Susan Musgrave

"Tihanyi ... gives us exquisite glimpses into the world ... encourages us to take the risk of love with the veils off, our eyes open."
—Ellen Jaffe

The poems in the book's final section "employ startling and beautiful metaphors.... These poems are unforced, unself-conscious, and deeply touching."
—*Canadian Book Review Annual*

About *Saved by the Telling*:

"*Saved by the Telling* is a fine work, full of colloquialism, personal in tone, and at times can straddle both the humorous and the serious with dexterity.... Tihanyi writes with lyrical grace and precision."
—*Windsor Star*

"Tihanyi's poems are vibrant and evocative in their revelation of the dynamic and very distinct patterns of women's lives; they speak to all women who live here and now."
—*Canadian Book Review Annual*

Photo: Constance Rennett

Eva Tihanyi was born in Budapest, Hungary, in 1956 and came to Canada when she was six. She teaches at Niagara College in Welland, Ontario, where she has lived since 1989. Tihanyi has published five poetry collections, the most recent of which is *Wresting the Grace of the World* (2005). *Truth and Other Fictions* is her first collection of stories. She is the literary editor of *In Retro* magazine, and for many years was a freelance fiction reviewer for the *National Post* and *Toronto Star*. She was also the first novels columnist for *Books in Canada* from 1995 to 1999. For discussion questions about this book, visit www.evatihanyi.com.